# Crossroads

# Crossroads

*a novel*

MATT ARNOLD

*Crossroads*

Published by Iceni Books®
610 East Delano Street, Suite 104
Tucson, Arizona 85705 U.S.A.
www.icenibooks.com

International Standard Book Number: 1-58736-321-6
Library of Congress Control Number: 2004103651

For everyone whose path has crossed mine over the years. I hope I left you a little richer for knowing me. And, in memory of my father.

# CHAPTER ONE

# A Secret

"Taylor, your father didn't really die in a car crash when you were a kid. He was killed. I had him killed." The weak, dying woman muttered this to her son as he sat perched by her hospital bed. He was leaning forward, straining to hear her words. Weak words from a weak and dying woman, lying emaciated in a hospital bed in a North Seattle suburb.

Taylor was stunned. He had prepared for the inevitability of her death for months now, but not for this. This came out of nowhere. The doctor had warned him that the cancer had spread to her brain and there would most likely be periods of dementia. Taylor's first reaction was to pass this bizarre comment off as such, but deep down inside it didn't feel right to him, especially since, in spite of her worsening physical condition, she had remained cognizant all through her illness.

A background of electronic beeps and hums enveloped them in the hospital room, empty except for Taylor Weir and his mother. He could barely hear her faint voice over the noise of all the machinery keeping her alive, monitoring her every function. He squinted out the window at the big billowy clouds moving slowly across the sky in a late January day, waiting for more to come.

Taylor had just turned twenty-nine the week before. Tall, with broad shoulders, he looked like he could be the younger brother of Johnny Depp. His hair was scruffy and medium length, dark. He had recently shaved off the hipster mustache and goatee he had kept for the last few years. He was quite handsome, he was often told.

It had been a hard few months for Taylor. What started out as lower back pain in his mother turned out to be a large, cancerous tumor nestled in her spine. Her family doctor had at first passed it off as lower back strain, but it only worsened with time. She stayed in bed with the misguided advice that keeping off her feet would heal it best. By the time the true nature of her pain was discovered it had spread to her lungs—and her brain. The doctors had given her a month to live and she had outdone that threefold. There was nothing they could do now except treat her pain. The cancer was too incorporated into her body, she was told. There were several failed rounds of chemotherapy and radiation treatment, but it was a constant downhill slide. They did little to stem the expanse of the disease, and only weakened her and made her sick. She had lost much of her hair in mangy-looking patches; she had lost a tremendous amount of weight; her eyes had become sunken deep in her gaunt, ashy face. The end was certainly close at hand.

She had been a good mother to Taylor, raising him alone in a small town twenty miles southeast of Seattle, Washington. He could not really remember his father. His parents had split up when he was a baby. He had first stayed with his father in the house he grew up in, but there had been a fatal car crash that claimed his father not too long after that. He was too young then to have any real memory of this. Taylor couldn't remember anyone really telling him about these early years, but he'd known all the details for as far back as he could remember. He had some vague remembrance of counseling during first grade. It must have been then that he learned of those early years of his life.

The death of his father when Taylor was two was what he told everyone had shaped his life. That was what set him apart from the rest of the world and made him who was. He stared at his ailing mother in stunned silence, waiting for her to continue. She closed her eyes and winced quietly in pain. Taylor waited patiently for this to pass. It always did.


When he was younger, first out on his own, he always worked it in early when meeting someone: "My parents divorced when I was one. I lived with my dad for a year, and then he was killed in a car crash. I can't even remember him. After that, my mom moved back in and raised me." It always gained him instant sympathy. Everyone had always thought him so troubled inside, so dark. It was not really his true nature, but it always seemed to make people interested in him. So he played the card. It wasn't till almost a decade later that he had the confidence to let it go and to allow people to meet the real him.

He always knew why he was a loner when he was younger. Although he had a lot of people to hang out with, he never really had any true friends. There were people he thought of as friends, but they always seemed to be coming and going, moving in or moving out of his life. This made such sense for someone who had first lost his mother, then his father. Even into his teens, he was never entirely sure if his mother was going to stay. The textbooks would have no problem explaining Taylor Weir.

No one really understood him, though. Although he rarely smiled as a child, he wasn't unhappy. He kept to himself but he wasn't lonely. He was a case study in the satisfaction of solitude. Actually, things in life had always really gone just the way he wanted. Or, more likely, he had learned to accept the way they ended up going. It is always hard to tell the difference. As he grew older he brooded less and less, spent less time alone, and became more "socially functional," as they say. He grew into quite a well-adjusted young adult, taking life as it came.


Realizing that his mother was dying was really the first time he'd had to deal with something that wasn't all right with him. He was having a tough time of it. Before now, nothing had been much of a problem for him.

Money had certainly not been a problem. His mother got half of his father's life insurance to live on. The other half was put into a trust fund for Taylor and grew untapped for sixteen years into quite a sizable amount. The '80s sure had been a boom time for investors. The interest off the trust was supposed to pay for his college and get him started after that. When he finished high school, very close to the top of his class, he sweet-talked his mother into letting him take a year off to figure out what he wanted to do. In high school he had loved the experience of learning, but had no clue of anything he really wanted to do for more than a semester, let alone the rest of his life. That's why he loved school so much: every few months, reset, and off to something new.

So Taylor convinced his mom to let him move out and got a tiny studio apartment in Seattle, in the

University District. The University is the University of Washington. Somehow he wondered if hanging around college students would help him to find something he wanted to do. Deep down inside, though, he knew that all he really wanted was to move onto something new. He just didn't know what that was yet. Living alone by The U, as the University of Washington is known, sure fit the bill. He was allowed to use the interest in the trust fund, which was more than enough for him to live on. The first six months were spent in a blur of excitement, out in the real world, more of an observer than a participant. This got rather boring after six months, so he agreed to take a class, and his mother, who still had control over the trust, agreed to pay for the tuition out of the principal so he could still live on the interest. His father's will had put her in charge of disbursement as long as she lived. His father hadn't put much thought into it, seeing his son as a baby and never envisioning him beyond that. Taylor was fine with this arrangement. His mother had been fair and seemed to be looking out for him.

She allowed him to draw off as much of the interest as he needed. It didn't seem to be too much money. His mother didn't realize that this was more than enough money. He really didn't buy anything outside of food and alcohol—lots of alcohol back in those early days on his own. And book, lots of books.

Taylor took an existential French literature class that first semester. This eliminated the boredom he had been falling into, exposing him to all sorts of wild mind-expanding books: Sartre, Camus, Ionesco, Beckett. He spent most of his time wandering around town with some deep, serious novel finding scores of sensory-enhancing venues to read his books. Just about the time he began to become bored with the class the semester drew to a close, and he finished off with the highest grade in the class. On the last day of class, the professor approached him and wished him luck.

Dr. Stoops chaired the Literature Studies Department at the University of Washington. He was a short man whose head was covered with wild curly hair; a scruffy beard obscured most of his face. The odor of clove cigarettes hung in the air around him at all times. Taylor couldn't imagine anyone as passionate as Dr. Stoops when it came to French literature. The day after a lengthy discussion about a Jean-Paul Sartre novel, when they talked about how the character's beard was a symbolic mask, hiding not only the physical form but the emotional form, Dr. Stoops arrived, cleanly shaven, to demonstrate just how much of a mask a beard could be. This had more impact on Taylor than the entire discussion the day before.

"You seem to have really connected to the class," Dr. Stoops told him on that last day of class. "Have you decided what you are going to major in? You might consider French Literature Studies."

Taylor was flattered. "I really enjoyed your class, Dr. Stoops. I'm still kind of up in the air about where I'm heading."

"Well, good luck. You're very talented, Taylor. Don't let it go to waste."

It was the first time someone whom Taylor respected had given him such a compliment. It wouldn't be the last. He felt it was well deserved.

With summer now upon him, his mother began asking all sorts of roundabout questions which all seemed to be simply "What are you going to do with yourself now?"

The deal they struck for the summer was that he could again just take one class, but he was going to have to get a job. She didn't feel like it was doing him any good to have a steady income without a job. It was too artificial and it wouldn't be healthy for him to think of this as normal. Expecting an argument, she prepared a long speech, at the end of which Taylor merely said, "OK." Actually, a job seemed just like another class, a new experience. He had, in fact, been thinking of the same thing. His mother was quite proud of him and relieved that there didn't have to be any conflict over it.

So, he took another literature class, this time Russian, and got a job pouring lattes at one of the million coffee shops off campus, Bean's. He was able to climb the steep barista learning curve in about fifteen seconds. Clearly he was going places. Even while making espressos, he was never seen without some book poking out of his back pocket. It was about this point that he began growing his hair out longer and began sporting one of those hippie goatees that seemed required for the neighborhood. He also began smiling a lot more. Summer quarter ended, and he again got the highest grade in his class. It seemed easy to him. He didn't understand why some of the other students struggled so much, although he gathered they weren't too interested in the class. Sometimes he appeared to be the only student in the class really interested; everyone else seemed to be just clocking time, filling a line on their transcript. Russian literature captivated him as much as the French class had, and he once again caught the attention of the professor, Dr. Boridovski. After Taylor turned in his final exam, Dr. B, as he asked his students to refer to him, approached Taylor and wished him well.

"I've enjoyed reading your insights into the material this semester. It has been a long time since I've had a student who really could see that deeply into it. You are quite perceptive, Taylor. Your name came up the other day when I was having lunch with Dr. Stoops. I was telling him about a student who really impressed me. He asked right away if it was you. You made quite an impression on him, too."

"Thanks, sir," Taylor responded.

"Have you considered majoring in Foreign Literature Studies?" he asked. "We have a good program here."

"I'm considering it," Taylor replied, not sure if it was really the truth, but wanting to be polite.

Fall quarter rolled around and again his mom probed for any semblance of a plan for his life. He still had none, but they did come to an agreement that since he was actually drawing less than the interest of the trust fund now that he was working, and as he was doing so well in school, things could just go on the same. She did remind him that at the rate of one class a quarter, he could expect his degree in fifteen to twenty years. He actually appreciated her sarcasm.


Life continued the same for some time. Every semester he took something new, something introductory, and worked at Bean's about twenty hours a week. The University's attitude was that as long as he paid, he could stay. After he had depleted the literature category— French, Russian, and German—he moved on to philosophy, psychology, history. In each he ended up near the top of the class and never received less than an A-. The professors all seemed to identify him as a gifted student. Often at Bean's one of his old professors would come in and talk with him as they got a coffee. He got the strange impression, at times, that they had come in to talk with him, more than to get coffee.

There was a certain thrill about the newness of the first day of class, and by the end of the quarter he was always willing to move on. Not really bored, but just filled. Because he was a part-time student he did not have an assigned guidance counselor who would have told him he had filled up, three times over, the humanity requirements for a degree, but had made less progress than a second quarter freshman at getting one. As though that was his plan, getting a degree. Actually, there was no plan. He was becoming quite intelligent and could hold his own in almost any subject. The people around the coffee shop considered him to be a fountain of knowledge and, more and more, he became surrounded by people who thirsted for this. He was their true renaissance hero, their bohemian.

He became a fixture at Bean's. Only Stan had been there longer than Taylor. Stan the man; Stan, the manager; Stan, the Deadhead. He had hired Taylor with barely more than a single question. The entire job interview consisted of Stan staring at him, asking just a question or two, and then remarking, "I have a good feeling you'll just work out fine." He was right. Taylor had now been working at the shop for almost four years, twice as long as anyone else. Most of the people who worked there hung out in the job for about a semester or two, then suddenly stopped showing up. Stan took care of all the hiring, all the scheduling, all the food and coffee bean ordering, all the paperwork. Actually, Stan did almost everything except make the lattes and ring the register. Stan was one of those people who was like an older brother to everybody. He always seemed to be bailing someone out of some jam, giving someone some advice. If Taylor did have anyone he would call a true friend, it would be Stan.

No one really knew how long Stan had been there. Whenever asked, he would just say "forever." He seemed to know everyone. One day an old friend of Stan's visiting from back East was hanging out with them at a pub after work, and Taylor heard enough to gather that Stan had graduated a decade earlier from Cornell, one of those Ivy League schools back East, and had moved out to explore the West for a year, which had turned into a lifetime. He certainly seemed a lot happier than his friend, who kept badgering Stan over the path his life had taken since they had graduated years ago. Taylor could tell that Stan's friend was really just jealous.

Stan was the one who turned Taylor on to the music that was referred to as "classic rock." Taylor liked rock and roll, and in high school had listened mainly to head-banger heavy metal music like Metallica, Guns 'n' Roses, AC/DC, and the like. He was quite disturbed at the lightening of the national music scene throughout the '80s and held strong that the guitar would not go the way of the dinosaur. Stan was always playing the Rolling Stones, the Who, Beatles, Dead, and stuff like that at Bean's, and they really began to grow on Taylor. They seemed to be the origins of the music he liked. Taylor also really liked the Seattle grunge music that was at first called "alternative" but later just became mainstream. If classic rock was the origins of the first music he liked, then grunge was its offspring. He saw a few of the bands in local clubs that would later go on to great fame and fortune. Years later, Taylor would tell people he was pretty sure he made a strung-out Kurt Cobain a vanilla latte once at Bean's, back when Nirvana was just a local band, unknown outside the Puget Sound area. He remembered Kurt saying "Thanks, brother" to him and tipping him a guitar pick. Taylor was very sad the day he heard Kurt had killed himself—it seemed like such a senseless loss. He was sorry he hadn't saved the guitar pick. It hadn't seemed important at the time.

Then one day at the end of May, out of nowhere, Stan vanished. Just a note on the fridge in the back storeroom: "Got a tip that this was going to be the last Dead tour, gotta go." Stan had told Taylor some real weird stuff, the night before he left, that this was his last chance to see the band. He kept alluding to all this New Age stuff about destiny, about things that were meant to be. None of it made sense. He figured it must have something to do with this new girl Stan had been seeing. Taylor had talked to her once, and she had seemed pretty intense, into all that New Age stuff. Stan joked about it behind her back at first, but pretty quickly took it real seriously, himself.

"Gotta go?" What the hell did that mean? The Grateful Dead had come every summer to Seattle, Tacoma, or Portland for a couple of shows for the last twenty-five years. Stan always caught all the Northwest shows. Taylor usually just went to the Seattle shows with Stan and some of their friends from Bean's. As a matter of fact, they had just seen back-to-back shows at the Memorial Stadium in Seattle Center the day before. The band was heading on to Portland, then on to California, apparently, with Stan in tow.

Stan seemed too serious about running Bean's to just up and leave. It was kind of like waking up one day to hear that the president of the United States had decided to quit his job and go on a yearlong surfing binge.

Now Stan was gone—the manager, gone. No one even knew who the owner of Bean's was. At first everyone figured Stan would be back, but after a few days it became clear that they had a problem. Because Taylor had been at the shop longer than anyone and hung out with Stan, everyone seemed to expect him to know what was going on. He was seen as Stan's best friend. There had to be a better explanation. They finally settled that there wasn't one—sometimes people just kind of weirded out.

Taylor was nominated to figure out what to do. Actually it was more like everyone else quickly professed that they didn't care and they were going to just stop coming in if no one could figure out how to pay them.

One day, not too long after this, Taylor went into the back office where Stan always seemed to be hanging out and poked around throughout the desk, through the filing cabinet, though the mountains of papers on the desk and on the floor. It didn't take him long to figure some basic stuff out. All the coffee beans came from one supplier and all the baked goods came from one bakery. He called both at the numbers on the bills he had found and confirmed that they simply came on schedule every Tuesday and delivered the same as the previous week unless told otherwise. When the woman at the bakery asked what was up with Stan, Taylor made up some vague story about a death in the family and a sudden trip out of town. After he hung up, he realized it was stupid to make up a lie. Why didn't he just say that he wasn't around? Already he felt himself covering for Stan. He figured that Stan would be back in no time and would greatly appreciate it.

For the rest of the month, Taylor put together the work schedules. He tried to pay the coffee distributor and the bakery with cash from the till, which they wouldn't take, so he ended up writing them personal checks and running to the bank and depositing the cash. The tellers seemed alarmed that he was depositing so much cash. He figured they assumed he was a drug dealer or involved in some other illegal venture. He paid all the employees in cash out of the till every Friday. They all seemed happy, like a bunch of sheep. The job seemed like a cinch. At the end of each week there was quite a bundle of cash left over in the register after everyone was paid. He bundled up most of it in rubber band rolls and stashed them in a shoebox under the desk in the back room. It was a vivid image of what was meant by profit. The whole thing seemed too easy. Stan had made it seem so hard.

After a few weeks, he was clearly in charge and Stan was merely a memory. Postcards arrived every couple of days from the road: first San Francisco, and then the band must have crossed the country because they were from Vermont, New Jersey, D.C., Indiana, Missouri, and finally Chicago, Illinois. At first the cards had pretty good descriptions of the shows but they began to make less and less sense. It was apparent that road was taking its toll on Stan. One card from New York City said "Nothing left to do but smile, smile, smile." Another said, simply, "Wow." It was from Chicago. The Dead had finished up their tour with three shows at Soldier Field, home of the Bears.

Cash was building up in the back room. Taylor had been in charge for about a month now and there was several thousand dollars stashed away. He was well aware that there must be more to running the place than he was doing, but things appeared to be going on fine. Deep down inside, he knew there was much he was missing, but he preferred the path of denial to the point where he convinced himself it was all under control. It really seemed too easy. He began to think that Stan's role really wasn't that big a deal.

Then, on the first day of the August, someone came in looking for Stan. Taylor thought it seemed like a cop, so he covered up for Stan. No he didn't know where he was. No he hadn't seen him for a while. No, he didn't know when he would be around. Finally the questions ended.

The guy unloaded on Taylor. "Look, I'm the owner of this place. Stan works for me. What the hell is going on? I got back from a few weeks in California and the bank is calling me, going crazy. No one is putting any money in

the account and there isn't enough to make the lease pay-
ment transfer this week. Where the fuck is Stan?" He
seemed to be getting somewhat agitated.

Suddenly Taylor thought of the cash in the back. It
wasn't profit at all. He spilled the whole story. The
owner, it turned out, was quite a nice guy. He quickly
calmed down. In addition to Bean's, this guy Ray owned
a few latte carts and a couple of student rental houses by
campus. Ironically, he had been down in California
catching the Grateful Dead shows and hanging out at the
beach. No, he hadn't run into Stan.

Ray was quickly impressed by how Taylor had kept
the place running and also relieved that things didn't
seem as bad as they could have been, under the circumstances. He did point out that there was a lot more to the
job than what Taylor had been doing. Ray said that Stan
did such a dependable job that the place seemed to have
been running on autopilot. He really didn't want that to
change. He was a hands-off owner and liked it that way.

Ray explained to him all the things he had to take care
of besides doing the schedules and paying the bills. There
was a mountain of accounting paperwork, employment
forms to file with the state, a bank account to manage. It
still seemed pretty easy. Taylor now understood why Stan
spent so much time in the back room with the door
closed. He had always assumed he was sleeping or getting
high. It turns out he was working back there.

Ray offered him Stan's job on the spot and Taylor
accepted it. The job became him well. His mother didn't
seem to mind that he was going to work full time since it
was obvious he was just taking classes for fun. Also, he
was making more money now and began using even less
of the trust fund interest.

So Taylor was made manager of the café, the new Stan. Jerry Garcia died at the end of that summer after the tour wound up in Illinois, so it turned out that Stan did catch the last Dead tour. Stan's last postcard, sent in September from Big Sur along the California coast, had no message, just a drawing of a blue teardrop.

The days blur into months blur into years. The little kid who lost his father becomes the manager of the coffee shop. He becomes such a fixture of Bean's that everyone starts calling him "Bean." He sees his twenties drawing to a close.

The years changed Taylor, slowly and subtly. Responsibility usually does that. He began to wear his hair a lot shorter and shave regularly. He became less of a loner, and much more outgoing. He had relationships a couple of times with girls he met at the coffee shop. Nothing real special, but the companionship was good for him. They were always students. They always graduated and moved on, fell out of touch. Regular hiking and exercise filled him out well. His body was slowly transformed from that of a skinny college student to a healthy, lean adult. The drinking tapered off into occasional adventuresome binges and the daily beer or two to unwind, all normal changes for the better.

Taylor now sat wide-eyed, at a total loss for words, staring at his mother, staring at the tubes coming out of her. She lay there emaciated from the cancer that had stormed her body with a fury just three months ago. Those last months had robbed her of nearly all semblance of the woman he had known. He couldn't believe how old she looked. She'd always looked so young before. A few years back she had celebrated her big five-oh. He remembered getting kind of drunk at the party and going on and on about how great she looked. Now she looked a hundred years old.

"I am going to die soon," she murmured. "You should hear the truth. Maybe I'll be able to go in peace, if there is such a thing."

He moved closer to his mother to hear. She could barely force enough air out to speak.

"What are you talking about, Mom? Dad died in a car crash. You know that."

"No, I paid someone to kill your father."

That was all he heard. She continued mumbling incoherently for some time, little tears streaking down her cheeks. He tried several times to communicate with her, but it appeared she could not hear him. Her mumbling began to fade out, until all was silent in the room except for the electronic noise of all the monitors. It all seemed so dramatic and surreal. He expected the heart monitor to flat line, releasing her for good, but life isn't always as dramatic as TV or movies. Instead, she lapsed into a coma for several days and slipped quietly away.

For Taylor, her life ended late one evening with a phone call from the hospital. The notification of the next of kin, as it is officially called.

She parted this world, but left her long-held secret behind.

Taylor sat up all that night, after the hospital had called to tell him that his mother had passed away. He felt reverberations going back though his entire life. He wasn't sure if it was the death of his mother or the newly discovered circumstances surrounding his father's death that was bothering him more. As he finally drifted off to sleep, he realized deep inside that it was obviously both. He felt very alone and confused in the world.

He had a dream that night, where his mom was alive and healthy. She was running all around the backyard of the house he grew up in. In the dream, Taylor was confused because he thought she was supposed to be dead. He tried talking to her, but she couldn't hear him. She was hanging clothes on one of those old-fashioned, outdoor clotheslines. The dream faded and merged into another, where he had somehow walked all the way to Hawaii and was hanging out on the beach drinking tropical drinks. Some surfer dude asked him how he had gotten across the ocean. He paused for a moment, and replied, "I don't remember, but, boy, am I sure glad to be here."

## CHAPTER TWO

# A Memorial

His mother had always been a vocal proponent of cremation and had never belonged to a church, so a funeral service seemed out of the question. Organized religion had done more harm than anyone to the belief in God, she had once said. Instead, there would be some sort of an outdoor memorial service where all those who cared for her could gather and pay tribute. That seemed in line with all the New Age stuff she was always into. During a moment of clarity, before she got too sick, she had described her last wishes to him. It was a morbid conversation at the time, but now he was glad they had it. It left no question about what he should do for a funeral. He had the unwelcome task of putting it all together and had not looked forward to this. It turned out to be pretty easy to set up.

Everyone who he had in mind to invite was already aware of her death and seemed to be expecting such a gathering. His mother must have shared her wishes with her friends because they were asking Taylor about it whenever they phoned him with their condolences. Most of her friends were in their fifties. Death was something they had not yet grown accustomed to, and that seemed to trouble many of them. He could tell it in their voices. She was the first of their group to go. It would not be the first funeral any of them would attend, but for many it would be the first funeral of a close friend. Because she had been sick, no one was surprised at her death, so he didn't have to deal with any shock on anyone's part. All Taylor had to do was make the calls; the rest would pretty much happen on its own.

First there was Jack, a recently retired Boeing engineer who had lived across the street from the house where Taylor grew up. He was the oldest of her friends, the only one who looked to be in his sixties, although Taylor had no idea how old he was. Jack had worked at the Boeing airplane assembly plant along Lake Washington, the same plant where Taylor's father had worked. Jack had lived across the street since before Taylor was born, never married. Taylor's mother and Jack had been close companions after the death of his dad. Jack was always coming over to do all the man things that needed fixing, lifting, or moving. Mowing the lawn, cleaning the gutters, things like that. When Taylor grew old enough to take these over, Jack seemed to come around less often, and his mother and Jack seemed to grow apart. In the past couple of years he hardly saw them together. But after Taylor's mom got sick, Jack was constantly by her side at the hospital. He seemed to be a comforting companion. Whenever Taylor came to visit his mom, he always seemed to interrupt some very private, hushed discussion. He had always wondered if they had been fooling around in the early days. Now he wondered whether his father's death was planned so his mother could be with Jack. That didn't seem too likely, but the thought did occur to him.

Besides Jack, there was Dorothy, Janice, and Maryanne. They were all parents of kids who Taylor had gone to school with since elementary school. Long after their kids grew up and moved away, they were still his mom's friends. They had formed a bridge foursome and played every Wednesday night for the last ten years, more talk then play. After she got sick, the bridge group disbanded. They had no one who could ever take her place at the table, understand all the subtle nuances of their game. Instead, the girls would all come together and visit his mom in the hospital. At first they would play bridge there, but as her condition worsened, this became impossible. Dorothy had told him a few weeks back that they were now playing Scrabble, a good game for three.

There was a smattering of other people who shared casual friendships with his mother, and all called to express their condolences and to let him know that they were interested in coming to the memorial. He had no idea how they all got his phone number. In all, it looked like about twenty people would show, none under the age of fifty.

He called the first listing in the yellow pages under cremation. It really didn't seem like there was any need to shop around. How could anyone be better or worse at creating a pyre? It seemed unlikely that one place would give him an urn of ashes while another would wind up giving him a partially-charred body and excuses of equipment problems. No, Abner's Crematory Services in Lake City seemed as good as any. All he had to do was sign some papers at the hospital releasing the body to them, and they took care of the rest. Little did he know that Abner saved money with batch processing, reducing to ash all the bodies to be cremated each day at the same time and dividing up the resultant pile of remains into the correct number of urns. It saved a tremendous amount of expense and boosted their profits significantly. Three days after the death of his mother, Taylor picked up an urn of her ashes—actually one-eighth her ashes and seven-eighths the ashes of others—and headed for the memorial service. "What he didn't know wouldn't hurt him" was their motto. That was true.

The service was being held in the morning at a small park along the Cedar River, a shallow river that ran through town where his mother had lived, a half-hour southeast of Seattle. It was the town where he grew up. It was a nice, sunny January day with a cold crispness in the air.

One by one his mother's friends showed up, sleep-walking like zombies into the park. They all seemed so old and sad, far beyond their true years. Jack looked a mess. The plan was to have a nice short get together with a moment of silence. Then, everyone was to toss some ashes into the river. In all, seventeen people showed up. Each person was actually going to throw one hundred-thirty-sixth of the remains of his mother, along with a mixture of seven other people. Little did they know that over the subsequent week his mother's ashes would be a participant in seven other ceremonies. She would be at the top of Granite Mountain in the Cascade foothills, tossed into the waters of Elliot Bay in Seattle, thrown out a plane over Vancouver Island in Canada, dropped from atop Seattle's Space Needle, and held in three different urns in various suburbs of Seattle.

The whole thing took about twenty minutes and seemed quite cleansing for everyone. Afterwards, every-one slowly trickled off to get back to their lives. Taylor overheard Dorothy, Janice, and Maryanne making plans to have lunch and go shopping. Jack remained back alone sitting on a bench, staring into the river. He looked extremely troubled and sad. Taylor noticed that Jack was wearing totally differently colored socks.

Taylor approached him slowly.

"Jack. Thanks for coming. We're all going to miss her," Taylor said quietly.

"Yeah, she was quite a friend to me all these years. I'm going to miss her."

Taylor paused for a moment with his mother's last words still fresh in his mind. He was sure of one thing: Jack must surely know a lot about it. He figured this might be a good chance to find out for himself what his mother was talking about.

"Did you know my dad? I can't even remember him," he asked Jack.

"Sure, I remember Jim. We worked at the same plant for a couple of years. Damn shame what happened to him. It must have been very hard for you growing up." Everyone always said that to Taylor.

Taylor was normally a pretty honest person. This was one time that he stretched that a little—actually he stretched that a lot. An idea popped into his head.

"You know, when I was cleaning out the house I came across a bunch of journals my mother kept. They go all the way back from before I was born."

"Really?" Jack suddenly looked like a deer caught in the headlights. More accurately, a deer that already had one foot in the grave, in the headlights.

"Yeah, I found out about a lot of things," he said with just the slightest hint of accusation, staring directly into Jack's tired eyes. "Don't worry, I'll keep it to myself," he said to Jack reassuringly. "The past is the past."

"Look, that was all a long time ago," Jack said.

"Just answer me one question. Do you have any regrets?"

"Taylor, of course I have regrets. I really didn't have a whole lot to do with her until after Jim died, but I always felt responsible. I don't know how I got sucked into the whole thing. After reading those journals, I guess you realize what kind of a woman she was back then. But she really changed over the years, she really did. Try to keep that in mind. I didn't figure out what was going on at the time. By then I was in love with her and there was no turning back. There was no way I could go back and change things. Look, I didn't do anything wrong. Out of respect for your mother's memory, let it go, Taylor."

Jack seemed on the verge of spilling his guts, but over what? What exactly had he done? His mother had said "I had your father killed." What was Jack talking about? Obviously he was probably the only one alive that knew what had happened. That seemed certain.

"Look, the stuff in her journals I read was vague. I think this was intentional. There is no way I can bring my father back. And Mom's dead. Any justice is being served in the afterlife I'm sure. I'll make you a deal, Jack. I deserve to know. That's all I want. That was my father. If you tell me what happened, I can let it go. I just want to know…I should know. That's not asking too much, is it? You didn't really do anything wrong, just a lot of stupid things. If they jailed for stupidity, there wouldn't be enough people left to be the guards. Hell, no one even cares about crimes going on today, let alone something that happened twenty-five years ago. I'm not into making any trouble." Taylor was rambling on as Jack gave him a somewhat puzzled look.

Taylor continued. "I know they weren't happy. Was it really that bad? And how the heck did my mom find someone to kill my father?"

Jack didn't even bat an eye at the mention of murder.

"Yeah, they weren't happy. Actually, your dad was perfectly happy and your mother was miserable. When they moved in next to me, your parents were the perfect couple. They made such a handsome pair, new baby and all. I never talked to them much. With your dad I must have had the same conversation after work at the mailbox a thousand times. I would always say "Howdy, how's it goin', Jim." Then he would say "Fine, how about your-self?" Not much for conversation it seemed. Just like me. But then, after about six months of this, I saw him one day at the plant. So many people worked at Boeing in those days that it isn't anything to work next to your neighbor. I saw him around a lot, but whenever we talked it was real superficial. Guy stuff. You know, sports, weather.

"He was always so good with you. I'm sure you don't remember that 'cause you were so young. I would always see him outside running around with you, doing something. You were quite an energetic kid, Taylor. I'll never forget this little car you had that you could ride in. He would push you all around the yard for hours. The wheels were always falling off it. He must have fixed the wheels on that car a million times. I think I have a picture around somewhere of you in that car. I'll have to look for it. I'll give it to you if I find it. It was strange, that I never saw your mother around.

He paused for a second, staring off into space.

"That was after about a year. I would never see her car around. And when she would show up your dad would take off right away. It was pretty easy to figure out what was going on. He came over collecting for some charity one time and I asked him how things were going. That's when he told me your mother had moved out. She was coming over before work everyday and taking you to day-care. Your dad would pick you up after work and bring you home and was living with you. She was also coming by a few nights a week. Your dad told me a lot more than I really wanted to know. It was all vague, none of my business really. A lot about your mother never being happy and moving out to find someone she could be happy with. He didn't seem to put up any fight at all since she agreed to leave you with him."

None of this was news to Taylor. "Look, I already know about all that. What I want to know is why she had him killed. I always thought things were working out back then. And how did you get involved in the whole thing?"

"About a year after your parents split up, your dad got a girlfriend. On the weekends when you were to be with your mom he would stay with his girlfriend and your mom would stay at the house with you. That was when I got to see her a lot. She was always coming over asking for help with things over at the house, or with her car. There always seemed to be something wrong with her car." He began to fidget like he didn't want to continue. "I think she was just lonely. So was I."

"So you and my mom were...uh." Taylor couldn't even say it. All he could think of was what his mom looked like when she was dying.

"Yes." Jack didn't even say it either. It was obvious. "She asked me over for dinner one night after I had spent several hours fixing the brakes on her car. There didn't seem to be anything wrong with going over since your parents had gotten divorced by then. She made a nice dinner. It was real platonic, the three of us eating. You must have been about two. We split a bottle of wine. After she tucked you in, we stayed up for hours, just talking. Things started to get more intimate. She was a very fascinating woman, you know. I guess it is hard for you to picture your mother as a beautiful young woman, but she was. I doubt you'll believe I was once a young, strong, handsome man. Just like you. Eventually it got real late and it was time to go. We kissed at the door for a long time. She kept whispering for me to stay, almost begging. I kept trying to cut it off and leave, but she kept pulling me in. Look, I'm not going to go into this."

It seemed so strange to Taylor to hear this kind of talk coming out of an old man. He suddenly was struck by the thought that he, too, would someday be that old. "You don't have to, I get the picture."

"Anyway, we fell in love and started spending a lot of time together. On weekends when you and your dad were at the house, I would go over to her apartment. She lived close by. The other times, when Jim was at his girl-friends, I would just hang out with you guys at the house. Everyone seemed happy about the arrangement, even your dad. He figured things out pretty quick. It wasn't really a secret, but we didn't want him to know. I think one of the neighborhood kids told him. Jim didn't seem to care. He stopped talking to me at work, though. Things got a little uncomfortable between us.

"It was your mom who started to get unhappy with the whole thing. She wanted to live with me and have you live with us. She started to have this fantasy that she would be happy for the first time in her life, the three of us living together. She knew your Dad would never go for it. He had legal custody of you in the divorce and she just had visitation. I started to get worried. She started becoming more and more obsessed. She was convinced she would become miserable unless the three of us could live together. I began to realize that I had made a huge mistake, but it was too late.

"Then she met my brother, Jason. He's in prison now, probably for the rest of his life, for murder. I never really knew Jason; I was in college when he was born. By the time he was a teen, it was real obvious he was not right in the head. Seems he got all messed up with drugs. He was in and out of school, in and out of juvenile hall, then in and out of jail. I think he's spent more time in jail than out. Anyway, he came by one day, all in a panic, needing money. He was all hopped-up on something and not making a lot of sense."

Jack seemed increasingly relieved as he continued the story. Taylor suspected he had probably never shared this with anyone and had carried it around inside for some time.

"Jason said he needed a thousand bucks to get out of town, but he could pay it back twofold within a week. He told me he was going to get ten thousand dollars for killing someone. I couldn't believe it, he just told me like that. Up till then he had pulled a lot of schemes and cons but nothing like this. Jason said he needed the money to get out of town that day and establish an alibi."

Taylor continued to listen, unsure what this was all leading up to.

"I didn't really believe him but I just wanted him out, I didn't want any trouble. The whole thing scared me, to be honest. He said he needed cash; he didn't want any locally canceled checks floating around. There was the implied feeling that if I didn't give him the money there'd be trouble. So I went to the bank and got him the money. Your mother must have heard the whole thing. She was there visiting when Jason came by, playing with you in my backyard. I went inside to talk with my brother in private, but she must have overheard it. It turns out while I was gone she made a deal with Jason to kill your father. He would get fifty thousand dollars, a few thousand up front and the rest from the life insurance. I didn't find this out till years later, only a few years ago, actually. I still can't figure how she worked it out so quickly with him. Jason went to prison, probably for the rest of his life, about five years ago. He got caught on a store camera killing two security guards during a robbery, then fell through the display window on the way out. When the police got there he was just laying in front of the store, bleeding and unconscious."

Jacks eyes dropped in sadness. The whole thing was obviously weighing on him.

"I felt obligated to visit him once he got sent away. He's in Walla Walla. He told me right away about killing your dad. I think he told me that just to hurt me. He knew about your mom and I. I guess you get that way when you realize you're in prison for life. I didn't believe him, but he had a lot of details about your mom that he shouldn't have known. I figured he was full of it at the time. After your mom got sick, she started bringing up a lot of things, things she said she was so sorry about, things way in the past. It never got specific. So one day I just blurted it out. It was obvious from the expression on her face that it was true. She didn't try denying it, she knew by then she was dying. She kept wanting to talk about it after that. She had kept it secret for all those years. We spent hours in her last days talking about it; she kept trying to figure out how she could have done it."

That explained all those hushed talks Taylor had often interrupted.

"I'm sure you were a big help to her," Taylor said. "I guess I never really knew her. I never had any idea."

"Taylor, you need to understand that your mother was not a well woman back then. But she did change. She became a great mother to you. That is the woman you knew, and that was real. This stuff, it happened so long ago. I think she truly didn't understand why she had done such a horrible thing. I think she made her penance by being so good to you over the years.

"After your dad died, things with your mom and I kind of fell apart. She inherited all this life insurance money and moved back in to your house across the street to take care of you. That all seemed to stress her out quite a bit, and it became harder and harder for her and I to have a good time when we were together. We did try for a while, but it became hopeless. I think it was the guilt of what she had done which really drove us apart. Being with me reminded her of what she had done, I guess.

"I still came over and helped with things around the yard, fixing things in the house, stuff like that. I was always good for that. But we didn't have much of a relationship. She was always so unhappy around me, but seemed fine around anyone else. That kind of hurt me."

Suddenly a bunch of little kids came flying through the park on bikes. Jack jumped with a start, looking disoriented for a moment. He looked meekly at Taylor.

"It felt real good to talk to someone about this." A hint of tears welled up in his eyes.

Taylor put his arm around Jack. He didn't know what to say. They sat there silently for at least ten minutes.

Finally, Taylor broke the silence. "Jack, it's all right. I shouldn't have brought this up now, not now, I'm sorry. I do really appreciate you sharing this with me."

"I hope it helped, for you to hear about it. It sure helped me to talk about it."

"Yeah, it helped a lot," Taylor said. "You take care of yourself. I'm going to have to deal with selling mom's house, so I'll probably see you around. Don't be a stranger."

They both got up to leave. There was a chill in the January air.

"If you ever need anything, like help fixing up the house or whatever, let me know," Jack said.

"Sure thing," he replied.

Leaving the park, they headed off in opposite directions. Taylor turned around and looked at Jack leaving.

He looked incredibly drained as he slowly crossed the park, his head bent down to the ground. Overhead, a flock of seagulls flew by.

Taylor felt exhausted. He had a sudden urge for a drink, actually many drinks. He got in his van and drove back to his apartment in Seattle.

## CHAPTER THREE

# A Bender

Bleary-eyed, Taylor looked up at the clock on the wall as he sat at the bar in a place simply called, "The Bar." It was the end of a long night.

"What the hell time is it," he thought to himself.

He took another swig of his tequila and OJ. He had been drinking all afternoon and into the evening at many different bars. It used to be a traditional journey of his, the "pub crawl," when he was younger. Over the last few years, it had become pretty infrequent. It'd probably been six months since he'd really tied one on. His mom's memorial service, and his talk with Jack, had wound him up so tight he needed the release.

He looked back on his day. After his mother's memorial service he had headed straight home. He felt trapped in his apartment, like he had to get out. He quickly drained the two beers that were in his fridge, thinking it would calm him down. Events of recent days were racing around in his head. He grabbed his jacket and headed out with no particular place in mind. Lost in his own zone, he headed along University Ave.

"The Ave," as it was known, ran along the edge of campus. The ten blocks from 40th to 50th Streets were lined on both sides with bars, restaurants, clothing stores, and coffee shops, all catering to students—in other words, all cheap. Bean's was dead center of The Ave on the corner of University Avenue and 45th Street. Taylor lived in a brick apartment building on the next street over, Brooklyn. He cut over to The Ave at the bottom 40th Street by the College Inn Pub and strolled along with no particular place to go.

He heard music blaring from somewhere up the street, a block or so ahead: the opening riffs of the Stones' "Gimme Shelter." Boy, did that beckon to him like voodoo. He headed towards the music; it was coming from a bar he frequented called the Palms. It was a time- less place, all dark wood inside, with booths along the walls and a huge mirror behind the bar. Music was always playing there, music he liked. He lowered his head and went in. The music was blaring, almost no one in the place. Not a surprise since it was only one in the after- noon. He bobbed his head to the music and sat at the bar.

"Whatta ya have?" the guy behind the bar asked him. How many times have bartenders uttered this line? This guy behind the bar was a tall, spindly character with long dreadlocks. He looked like he'd passed most his life per- fecting the art of hacky sack.

"Pint of Redhook," Taylor responded. Mick Jagger was screaming about war and love. "Man, what a tune," Taylor thought to himself.

The music hypnotized him like black magic. He looked up and there was a beer in front of him, as if out of nowhere. He didn't even notice the bartender putting it there. He took a deep gulp. The beer tasted great, much better than the Smidtz's Ice he had at home. To make his buck stretch, he was going for price performance on the home front. He drank his beer and listened to the tunes.

The music faded, then "Love in Vain" droned through the bar. He had found a good place to spend the afternoon, at least for now. The Stones' Let it Bleed was one of his favorite albums of all time. The bluesy riffs of the song perfectly matched his mood at the moment. He drank on, swaying to the music. Suddenly he realized his glass was empty. He had a nice healthy buzz on. He was the only one in the place, except for a couple in the corner who sat stone-faced and silent while they ate their meals. They didn't look too happy.

Taylor looked around for the bartender. He caught a glimpse of him through the back door of the bar, out back in the alley smoking something, a cloud of smoke enveloping his head. After a few minutes, the back door burst open and the bartender came jive walking in to the music and shouted, loudly, "I got nasty habits!" to no one in particular.

Noticing he had abandoned his sole patron, he made his way up to the bar.

"This is about my favorite album of all time," Taylor said to him, hoping to strike up a conversation.

"Have one on the house." Taylor's glass was instantly refilled to his utter amazement. In his entire life, he had never had one "on the house." He thought that only happened in the movies.

The bartender reeked of dope and had a somewhat crazed look in his eyes. He began cutting up lemons for the heifeweizen. In the zone, he picked up each lemon, sliced it up in seconds, and tossed the pieces into a bowl. He must have cut up dozens in a minute. The music seemed to drive him. Then, of course, the obvious happened. Taylor could see it coming. With a great yell and a large splash of blood, the knife cut into the bartender's palm just as Mick Jagger sang "You can bleed on me." Taylor and the bartender both laughed wildly. Is anything weirder than real life? The wound didn't seem too serious.

"Man, I hate when that happens," the bartender said as he wrapped a bar rag around his hand. He seemed fine. "Hey, you look familiar; you work at up the street at Bean's, don't you?"

"Yeah, I run the place." Taylor always loved the sound of that.

"I was a good friend of Stan's. What the hell ever happened to him?" the bartender asked. "He just up and vanished."

"Last I heard, Stan was following the Dead around on that last tour. We never really heard from him after that. I guess he quit. I haven't heard from him in years."

"He was pretty cool. I'm Chris."

"Chris, glad to meet you. I'm Taylor." Chris must have been quite stoned because he hadn't even noticed that the bar rag had fallen off his hand and blood was dripping down onto the floor. Taylor kept working on his beer; this second one was almost done.

Suddenly Chris looked down at his bleeding hand. "Yikes, I guess I'd better deal with this." He fashioned a crude bandage out of a clean bar rag and some duct tape that was behind the bar. It looked pitiful. "Good thing about pouring in a tavern, you only really need one hand," he said with a dopey smile, waving his unbandaged hand up in the air. Taylor finished his beer just as Chris tripped over the overflow beer bucket, spilling several gallons of beer all over the floor.

"Fuck, this is NOT my day." Chris headed to the back and returned with a mop. He mopped up the beer, and when he looked up he noticed that Taylor's glass was empty. "Man, if you want another, just reach over and fill it up. But no more on-the-house. OK?"

Taylor reached his glass over and refilled it from the tap. "Gotcha," he said to Chris. Taylor got a kick out of how spastically Chris was mopping up the beer. Taylor was so enthralled he didn't notice that the glass he had been filling from the tap, as he leaned over the bar, was overflowing. The pint glass slipped out of his hand and shattered on the floor. Thinking of nothing else to say, he shouted, "Banzai!" Chris was dancing around wildly to the music: "Monkey Man." He was yelling, "I'm a monkey man!" Things seemed somewhat out of control for late afternoon, but this was a dive bar, and that's what he came in here for.

A longhaired hippy-looking guy came into the bar. In perfect timing, he yelled out with the music, "All my friends are junkies." He looked at Chris behind the bar; it was a total mess. "Hey, Chris, what the hell is going on?"

Chris looked up. "Hey Phil, what the HELL is going on, you're twenty-four hours late. I had to work your shift yesterday."

"Yesterday? No way. I was off yesterday. Definitely. I specifically asked for Monday off."

"Phil, today is Wednesday, yesterday was TUESDAY you moron. Now get back here and help me clean up this mess. I totally spazed out, as you can see, and made a freakin' mess."

Let it Bleed was coming to an end and it was time to go. Phil and Chris were putting the bar back into order. Taylor got up and said, "Chris, see you around, sorry about the mess. Come by Bean's sometime and I'll give you a freebee." He left a ten on the table and walked out as "You Can't Always Get What You Want" was fading out.


The late afternoon sun blinded him. He put on his cheap sunglasses. That helped. He headed up the street; this time, he had a place in mind: Dunbar's. An "authentic"

Irish bar, if there could be such a thing outside of Ireland. He walked into the bar just in time to hear a guy up front playing the opening of Skynard's "Freebird" on a bagpipe. Happy hour must have started. The place was pretty crowded, not like the last place. He got a pint of Guiness. What else would you get in an Irish pub? The bagpipes blared on unrecognizably. He thought for a minute he heard a clip of "Sweet Home Alabama."

"My god, a bagpipe Skynard melody…can't be," he thought to himself. People were dancing around up front by the stage to the bagpipes; the music appeared to have absolutely no rhythm, but that didn't seem to matter. He drank his beer and took it all in. He spotted a few people he casually knew, no one by name, just people from around campus and Bean's. He finished his stout and ordered a tequila and OJ. "Goodbye, mom," he mumbled to himself as he drained half the drink in one gulp.

Suddenly the bagpipe blew apart at the seams with a horrifying noise, followed by total silence. The crowd roared with laughter. Apparently the music show was over. The guy playing the bagpipe sulked off with his dead music bag in his hand. Someone yelled, "You suck!" at the top of their lungs.

Taylor finished his drink and headed for the door. On the way out of Dunbar's he bumped into a friend of his who was on his way out. Taylor couldn't quite remember where he knew the guy from.


He was feeling pretty lightheaded. He crossed the street and went into Mexacali's. The tequila went down fine, but tequila in an Irish pub just didn't seem right. A Mexican bar was more like it. Behind the bar was a gorgeous blond-haired female bartender with a tight, low-cut shirt. Taylor couldn't help staring at her breasts. Suddenly he realized she was talking to him.

"Can I help you?" she said with an air of annoyance.

He thought of delivering the line a friend of his had always dared him to try: "That's a nice blouse. Why don't you take it off?" Instead he just ordered a double tequila and grapefruit. He took his drink and sat down by the window, watching the sun go down. He nursed his drink and enjoyed the beautiful sunset. His drink tasted like water. Suddenly, it occurred to him that he had a lot to think about. Somewhere, the thought of driving to the prison in Walla Walla and talking to Jack's younger brother hatched in his drunken mind. He wasn't sure why, but it seemed like a good idea. He was lost in thought— tequila 'n' thought. Sounded like a country song.

He looked up at the clock again: six o'clock. Where had the time gone? It had been just barely past noon when he had headed out of his apartment. He got up to leave and, just as he turned to go, his eyes met those of the most captivating woman he had ever seen. He fell back into his chair. He'd seen her around from time to time, but couldn't really place from where. Everything about her was dark: her clothes, her hair, her eyes. She was staring right into his eyes. It was freaky. He smiled at her but she just looked at him with a blank look. He was caught in her daze. She started walking towards him, never taking her eyes off him. She appeared to float rather than walk. He realized he was pretty drunk. She walked right up to him and said in a deep, husky voice, "You're a friend of Stan's aren't you? Where did he ever disappear to?" Taylor could smell alcohol but he wasn't sure if it was from her or from himself.

Then he remembered where he had seen her before. She was this New Agey girl who worked at the incense shop a couple of blocks down from Bean's. Stan had pretended to be all into incense and spent about $50 at the store with the sole intent of sleeping with her. He would come into the coffee shop with sticks of incense in his hand and just throw them in the garbage on the way in. It must have worked because one time Taylor had stopped by Stan's to pick up a couple of CD's, and this girl was coming out of his bedroom with one of his t-shirts on. On her, it hung down to below her knees. Her name was something like Ginga, but he figured her real name was probably real white bread like Ginger. She was the one that Stan was going out with right before he bolted.

"I don't know. Last I heard he was following The Dead on that last tour. I haven't heard from him after that." Taylor was having difficulty making coherent speech and he wasn't sure if she'd understood a single word he'd said. She stared right into his eyes. It was freaking him out. Also, she was real sexy, and Taylor began daydreaming about her. He was thinking that she must have black bra and panties on.

"Stop that," she said.

"What?" he said.

"You know what." Stan had got kind of freaked out by her in the end and told Taylor that she had all these clairvoyant powers. Reading Taylor's mind at this point when he was leering out at her would hardly constitute psychic power. It did kind of jolt him, more out of getting caught and put in his place than anything else.

"Tell me my fortune," Taylor said somewhat sarcastically, although it came out all slurred, more like "Hell to me in torture."

She laughed at him. It was the first time she'd broken out of her blank expression. He wasn't sure if he was going to get a fortune or a torture. In his state, and with her, he'd be up for either.

"Oh, I'll tell you your fortune, coffee boy." She seemed drunk.

"That's coffee MAN," he said. He always had the comeback for any line.

"Buy me a drink; I'll tell you your fortune," she said. She seemed to have lightened up tremendously.

Taylor went up to the bar and ordered another double tequila and grapefruit, then suddenly realized he had forgotten to ask her what she wanted. Being a woman, white wine was a fair guess, but she looked pretty tough. She didn't seem like the white wine type. He caught her eye and was able to mouth, "Hey, what do you want?" She was saying something but he couldn't make it out. Then, inside his head, he swore he heard a voice say "Gin and tonic." Man he was drunk. He walked over to her and asked her what she wanted.

"Gin and tonic. Didn't you hear me?" she said with a smile.

He went back and got the drinks. He made hers a double too. He was kind of horny and Stan had said she was a wild woman in bed.

He put her drink in front of her.

"Why, thank you kind sir," she said.

"I'm sorry, I don't remember your name. I was working for Stan when you guys were going out. Actually, I took Stan's job when he bolted. I'm Taylor."

"I remember your name. I'm great with names. I'm Ging." It rhymed with ring. "You don't have to look at me so strangely. I don't bite."

"I'm sorry, it's been a real long day," he said.

She guzzled the drink down in a matter of minutes and held the empty glass in front of her, looking at him vampishly. "Gonna buy me another?"

Obviously, he had no choice. He was only half done with his. Not wanting to get out of synch, he finished his off in one gulp and went to the bar and ordered two more. He didn't get doubles this time.

They talked for a while. It turned out she still worked at the incense shop down the street from Bean's. Taylor was amazed he hadn't seen her in all this time.

He was in a good mood so he didn't bring up anything about his mother or father. He told her about how he had been taking classes and working at Bean's and how, after Stan left, he started working full time. She told him she had moved to Seattle from Europe when she was two. Her parents were Romanian. She told him she was technically by blood an actual Gypsy. Her parents had moved to Southern California after she graduated from high school, and she had stayed behind, living in Seattle. She actually seemed a lot more normal than he expected. Ging didn't talk about New Age stuff or anything like that. Instead, they talked about places in the city where they had lived and hung out. It turned out they had a couple of mutual friends besides Stan. They finished their drinks and she offered to buy another round. They seemed like two long lost barflies. He felt a strange, instant connection to her. She seemed incredibly interesting to him.

"Gee, let me think," was his response to her offer. "Well, OK," he said, with the twisting of the arm behind the back that must have been done by the first caveman asked such a question.

Taylor had an almost unlimited tolerance to alcohol. They drank and talked small talk for a while.

"You know, I'm the one who told Stan to go on the Dead tour, that it would be the last one," she said, almost out of nowhere, with a hint of bragging.

"Yeah, who would have guessed? Jerry Garcia, dead before his time," he replied.

"Lucky guess? Is that what you think?" she said kind of smugly as she polished off what Taylor thought was her third, or possibly fourth, drink. She couldn't have weighed more than one hundred pounds. He couldn't tell if she was mad at what he had just said.

"I'm sorry. I didn't mean anything by that, really." He was already thinking that if he played it right, he might be sleeping with her in no time. Anyway, she seemed kind of nice, and he didn't mean to give her crap. They were both pretty drunk.

She got up and, without even asking him, went to the bar and got two more drinks.

When she returned, Taylor took a long draw on his drink and blurted out, "Tell me something about me."

"Are you sure? I'm for real, you know."

He was drunk enough at this point to just go with it. She took a deep breath then simply said, "He's not dead."

"Who?"

"You know who."

All Taylor could think of for some reason was Jerry Garcia. They had been talking about him earlier. Jerry was most certainly dead.

"What are you talking about?"

She finished her drink and got up and went to the bar. She returned, this time with a shot of tequila and a shot of vodka. She put the tequila in front of him. She downed the shot of vodka and gave him a sad look.

"Your father, he's not dead," she said as she got up, turned, and walked out of the bar.

Taylor was totally stunned. Things had been going perfectly one minute, and then she was gone. What a crazy thing to say. God, no wonder Stan was afraid of her. This girl was a freak. His drunken reactions were so slow that by the time he got up and ran out after her, she was gone. He went back in and sat down. It was funny how things seemed so real when you're drunk. He picked up the shot of tequila and drank it down. His first thought was that he guessed he wasn't going to get laid tonight after all. Then he thought back to what she had said about his father. He didn't know what to make of it. He figured he must have talked about it without remembering.

He got up and headed home. It was still early, only around eight. He backtracked on his way home, a favorite habit of his. A stout at Dunbar's, a Redhook at the Palms—even for him, this was adding up. Across the street from the Palms was an old-timer's bar just called "The Bar." He swaggered up to the bar and ordered a tequila and OJ. His vision was beginning to blur, a good sign that he should think of calling it a night. He was only a couple of blocks from home. It was getting late. He nursed his drink and thought over the night. The encounter with the psychic girl—he couldn't remember her name—was a blur. Had she really told him his dad was alive? He remembered Stan swearing she was for real. He also remembered Stan saying something vague about how he had to go follow the Dead because it was going to be their last tour. He seemed so sure of that. At the time, Taylor had thought Stan was just wigging out and was full of it. Taylor sat on his bar stool. He looked up to see what time it was, but found he could no longer read the clock. That translated into time to go home.

He finished his drink and left. He negotiated the complicated sidewalk the several blocks home. He couldn't find his keys and spent about a minute swearing to himself about how stupid he was, then suddenly he found his keys lying on the floor in front of him. They must have fallen out of his pocket. He staggered up the stairs to his apartment, opened the door, and laid down fully-clothed right inside the door and fell asleep, barely able to even close the door.

# CHAPTER FOUR

# Prison Visit

Taylor awoke in the morning on the floor just inside his door, fully clothed, his head pounding. He could not focus his eyes enough to see the clock on the wall but he could see daylight outside. "It must be morning," he thought to himself. He lay on the floor and looked at the refrigerator, a mere thirty feet away. It might just as well been a million miles. There was water, ice-cold water, inside it. He was well aware of the dehydrating effect of a long drinking binge and the miraculous powers of water. Rising first on one knee and then bringing himself upright with a large moan, he limped his way to the kitchen. He opened the fridge and peered inside. "Fuck," he said to himself, seeing the large gallon jug of water with only a few mouthfuls left. He picked up the jug and drank what little water it had. He filled it up in the sink and walked around the apartment, carrying the plastic one-gallon milk jug full of water. Already he was feeling clearer. He took four aspirins, hoping they would quiet the pounding in his head.

He walked to the bedroom and took off all his clothes, taking a swallow of water after each article of clothing was removed. Then he headed into the bathroom and took a long, steaming-hot shower. He imagined the water soaking into his pores, invigorating him.

While he was brushing his teeth in the sauna that the bathroom had become, he heard the phone ring. He ignored it, that's what answering machines are for. He could just make out the muffled voice on the recorder; it sounded important.

Taylor got himself dressed and already felt like a totally recovered man. For the first time since awakening, he looked at the clock: two in the afternoon. He wasn't sure what day it was, but Thursday was his guess. He had already told everyone at Bean's he wouldn't be in the rest of the week. They all understood. Unlike Stan, who insisted on doing everything himself and becoming totally indispensable, Taylor had at least two people lined up for each major task he had to do. So, it was no problem to take a couple of days off.

There were a couple of messages on the answering machine, all from a Mr. Evans from the bank. Taylor suddenly remembered a couple of messages from the bank earlier in the week right after his mother died, all asking him to call. He had totally forgotten. Now the messages seemed a little more urgent. He wrote the number down on the back of a piece of junk mail. He didn't feel like dealing with it now; it obviously had to do with the trust fund that his mother had managed. Taylor wanted to just keep it alone, just drawing off what he needed and letting the rest ride. He wasn't sure if he could do that, but his guess was that the bank would be more than glad if he left the money with them to manage.

He returned Mr. Evans call hoping to just leave a message, a poor excuse for dealing with the matter. When the voice at the other side said, "Good afternoon, Steve Evans here," he hung up. He didn't want to deal with this now; he had other things on his mind. He stuffed the envelope with the number into his back pocket. He'd call later and leave a message.

Looking back on the last night, it was all pretty much a blur. He did remember the psychic girl telling him that his father was still alive. He wouldn't have given it a second thought if it weren't what Stan had said about her. Stan was convinced she was for real. He'd never really explained why he thought this, he'd just given a lot of vague references to stuff she'd told him. Taylor had no idea how she could have known that his father was dead, but he figured there was a good chance Stan had told her about that. And the way she told him to stop fantasizing about her, well, that was hardly clairvoyant. But the whole thing was on his mind.

Taylor felt suddenly drawn to find her and talk to her some more. He was confused how things could have been going so well with her and ended so strangely. Chalk it up to alcohol, he thought. He definitely had the urge to ask her out.

He made a pot of coffee and toasted a bagel. Time to think. In the middle of his drinking binge the other night he had decided he was going to drive out to Walla Walla and visit Jack's brother, Jason. Usually ideas that were hatched and pickled in alcohol were quickly dispatched away the next day, but this one still seemed solid. What could it hurt? He had until Monday off work, with no plans. Walla Walla would make an interesting road trip, perhaps it would answer some questions, bring closure to the whole thing, and he could go on with his life.

Suddenly he smelled something burning. For the millionth time in his life, he had put a bagel in the oven broiler and forgot about it, and now it was burnt to a crisp. He hated how this always happened, yet he never seemed to go out and buy a toaster. He threw the burnt bagel into the trash and poured himself a cup of coffee. He was feeling much better by now and figured he needed at least a little to eat. He opened up the fridge and grabbed an orange—that would hit the spot.

While drinking his coffee he got out his Washington State road map. He knew most of the state like the back of his hand but he rarely went over the Cascades to Eastern Washington. It was pretty clear how to get there, all freeway. I-90 over the cascades to Ellensburg, a rodeo town with a state university, Central Washington University. From Ellensburg, another major freeway, 82, went through Yakima and on to Tri-Cities. From there it looked like there was another main road that went on to Walla Walla. The first part of the drive he had done many times, over the mountains and into the desert. But he had never veered south like he was going to. He assumed it was just going to be endless desert driving at high speeds. His map had the state penitentiary marked; it was on the northwest corner of town.

He suddenly got the urge to leave immediately and get the whole thing over with. If he waited, he thought he'd probably lose his nerve. He loaded up food for the trip: a large jug of water, a box of granola bars, a couple of protein-juice drinks, and a bottle of vitamins. He felt fine but he wasn't sure if he was up to any real food yet. At least the pounding headache and massive dehydration were gone.

He got his stuff together for the trip: some extra clothes, a sleeping bag, and a six-pack of Guinness Stout in case things got boring. As he was putting it all in a pile, he could hear all sorts of commotion out in the hallway. Out the window he suddenly noticed a whole slew of emergency vehicles: an ambulance, an aid car, a police car, and a fire truck, lights ablaze. This was a regular occurrence. This whole team showed up at least three times a month to deal with something in the apartment at the end of the hallway. There was a middle-aged couple who lived there. Dale and Sharon, their names, was all he knew about them.

The first time this happened Taylor got a little freaked out and figured one of them was dead. It was quite scary, but after about an hour everyone left and no body, dead or alive, was taken with them. The paramedics were grumbling on their way out, which didn't seem very professional. Taylor knew nothing about Dale and Sharon—even that was just from the names on the mail that had once been put in his box by mistake. He never got the nerve to ask them what had happened.

Then the ambulance came a second time. It didn't seem as much of a big deal this time, and was a repeat of everyone in, everyone out an hour later, grumbling. No Dale or Sharon being taken away. Taylor didn't even know which one needed the 911 call. From then on, every couple of weeks the same thing happened. This had been going on for at least a year now.

Taylor headed out with all his stuff. The paramedics were leaving Dale and Sharon's. As they passed him, Taylor heard one say to the other, "Fuckin' panic attacks..." Uniformed people began streaming out of the apartment: policeman, fireman, aid man. Taylor suddenly thought of the circus act with clowns piling out of the Volkswagen beetle. The cop bumped into Taylor in his sudden rush to get out and knocked everything out of Taylor's hands. The cop didn't even miss a step. He just kept walking past, leaving the mess behind him. Taylor thought this might be because the guy heard the smashing bottle and didn't want to stop and deal with it. He had already had his share of hassles with Dale and Sharon down the hallway. Only one casualty, that still left him with five. While he was cleaning up the mess, the hallway quickly emptied of people and was suddenly quiet. He could hear Dale shouting at Sharon as the fire truck pulled away, but couldn't make out any of it. As he made his way down the stairs, heading for his car, he finally heard Sharon unload back.

Washington State changes by the minute when leaving Seattle going east. The Mount Baker tunnel separates the city from Lake Washington. Past the tunnel, the I-90 bridge crossing over Lake Washington leads to the East Side, the California of the northwest, for better or for worse. The East Side, as it is known, is a collection of towns, across Lake Washington from Seattle, which were rural farmland until a building explosion of the 70s and 80s. Within fifteen minutes, the freeway begins to climb into the Cascade Mountains. Taylor had climbed all the mountain peeks that lined the freeway: Tiger Mountain, Mount Si, Granite Mountain, McClellun Butte. He'd been on top of all of those so many times he had lost count. From the top of these peaks are incredible 360-degree panoramic views as far as the eye can see. The freeway crests at three thousand feet at the Snoqualmie Pass, with ski areas on either side. Then, there's the big descent down into Eastern Washington. Within thirty minutes the mountains are a memory, and suddenly it is desert everywhere. At Ellensburg he turned south and headed towards Tri-Cities. The only thing this area had been known for was the Hanford Nuclear Site. Beyond Ellensburg, it was desolate, high-speed driving. He'd been on the road non-stop for almost five hours. He was almost there and was beginning to realize that he wasn't very well prepared. Before he had much time to think, he passed a road sign: Walla Walla was twenty miles away. Before he got to the city, there was a turn-off labeled "Walla Walla State Penitentiary." He took the exit and within minutes was in the parking lot of the prison. It was unmistakable, the large barbed wire walls with guard towers on each corner. He followed the visitor sign, thinking right away of how, as a kid, he would sing "just visiting" when landing on the jail in Monopoly.

One thing was immediately clear: something was going on. There were at least a hundred people in the parking lot, yelling and screaming. Many were holding signs. Tension was in the air. The mass was divided into two equal groups separated by about fifty feet and around twenty policemen. Taylor was pretty quick to figure it out. It was just a matter reading the signs. On one side were "Die, child killer, die," "Go Straight to hell," and other rather bloodthirsty slogans. The other side had "Two killings do not make a right," and "God forgave us, why can't we forgive," amongst others. The place was a mob scene, ready to explode. Taylor didn't pay much attention to the news, but the scene was enough to refresh his memory: the long-awaited execution of Randy McMullin. Taylor didn't remember any of the details except that McMullin had killed a young child, and the details were supposedly so gruesome that several of the jurors had nightmares for years. McMullin had put up very little fight at his trial, was quickly convicted, and waived all appeals after sentenced with the death penalty.

This was obviously not the day to visit the state pen. Taylor did a quick U-turn and headed away from the prison with no plan in mind. In his rearview mirror he could see the two groups faced off across the heavily guarded no-man's land. He figured by this time tomorrow McMullin would be dead, and all these people would return back to their lives, mistaken that they had somehow had an impact on the whole thing. Taylor was glad McMullin would be dead for what he had done.

He got back on the freeway skirting the north end of the city and headed east following a sign for Waitsburg; he'd come back tomorrow. Within minutes, he was out in the desert. Taylor took the first exit, went far enough down the road so that he'd not be visible from the freeway, and pulled off. He was on a small ridge with a perfectly unobstructed view westward. He ate two granola bars, a couple of cheese sticks, and washed it down with a protein-juice drink. Sunset was still a couple of hours off, and Taylor spent the time playing an acoustic guitar that he had brought along. When the sun dipped down in the west he opened one of his Guinness Stouts. He had kept them in a cooler with just a little ice to maintain them at a perfect, cellar temperature. He drank stout and watched the sun go down, all alone. It was a gorgeous desert sunset that seemed to last forever. By the time the last trace of color had left the sky, he'd finished three of the stouts and felt a sense of total peace. While he often achieved this feeling, he realized many people went their whole lives without experiencing anything close to this.

In the light of the first quarter moon, Taylor unrolled his sleeping bag and lay down under the stars; he was asleep within minutes. He awoke just as the first rays of the rising sun were reflecting off his car onto his face. It was a good night's sleep. He quickly got his things together and headed back to Walla Walla. On the drive he ate his breakfast of granola bars and washed them down with another protein-juice drink.

What a difference a day had made. The parking lot was completely empty. Apparently all the protestors were gone. Taylor assumed the execution had gone on as planned. The only thing every one would be able to agree upon was that they'd hope to go their whole lives without crossing paths with someone like McMullin. Taylor followed the signs to visitor parking.

Right away the signs of authority were all over. First he came to a manned gate. He told the guard there that he had come to visit someone. That didn't seem to be enough. The guard wanted to know whom he was seeing and asked for ID. He handed him his driver's license and told him he was there to see Jason Sanderson. The guard went back into his station and typed into a computer. A few minutes later, he gave Taylor his driver's license back and a printed pass. "Keep the pass on you at all times, sir," he said as he waved him on.

This wasn't the end. There was a fenced in parking area where he had to leave his car and a single door that opened to a small lobby just inside the main wall of the prison. He passed through a metal detector that was built into the doorframe. Another guard there looked at the pass and asked again whom he was there to visit, even though it was on the pass. Taylor calmly said, "I'm here to see Jason Sanderson, sir." The guard seemed to like the "sir" and told him to take a seat. The guard went to the phone and spoke into it for several minutes in a dry, military fashion. After about ten minutes the phone rang and the guard answered it, listened for a minute, and then said simply, "OK." He gave the pass to Taylor and pointed towards a small door at the end of the room. It buzzed, and the guard opened it up and motioned him through. There was a long hallway with another door on the end. He suddenly wished he was back in Seattle. He waited for a moment outside the door at the end of the long hallway, then there was a buzz and it opened into another room. This is what he expected. This room looked like the prison visitor room he'd seen many times on TV or in movies, a long glass wall with desks paired-up on opposite sides of the wall, each with a phone. A guard looked at his pass and pointed towards a young, tough-looking guy with tattoos up and down both arms.

"There he is," he said to Taylor.

Taylor sat in front of the man he assumed was Jack's troubled little brother, and began speaking to him. He recognized him as the hoodlum he'd sometimes seen from across the street, coming and going from Jack's a couple of times a year. It had been a couple of years since he'd last seen him. Taylor had figured him to be a long estranged son of Jack's rather than a younger brother.

"Jason Sanderson? I'm Taylor Weir. I got something I need to talk with you about." He was real nervous. He looked up and Jason was looking at him with an annoyed look on his face, waving the phone in the air. Taylor had been talking into the glass. He picked up the phone and talked again.

He was almost immediately cut off: "What do you want?" Jason said. He sounded more annoyed than tough.

Taylor didn't really know where to begin. "Look, I'm a friend of your brother's. I need to talk with you about something."

"OK, but I'm pretty busy. I think I might get out of here in thirty or forty years and I still have a bunch of things to get done." Taylor didn't expect any humor. "You a reporter or something?"

"No, a private investigator," Taylor said. It seemed really easy to lie to someone who would spend the rest of his life behind bars. How could this guy know the difference? "I'm looking into something from a long time ago. You might be able to help me." He sat up straight, stared right into Sanderson's eyes, and spoke in a clear strong voice. Taylor had read an article for an introduction to psychology class that said that eye contact, posture, and tone of voice defined the elements for obtaining control in a conversation. It seemed to work because the response wasn't the "fuck you" he had feared.

"Why should I help you," was Jason's response.

"Why not?" Taylor said simply. He didn't think there was any danger of this decaying into a back and forth childish argument of why and why not thrown from one to the other. "Look, I'm working for someone who's being charged with a murder that he had nothing to do with. He looks guilty as hell and he'll probably go to jail. I have several people that told me you did it. I can keep you out of it if you give me something that can get this guy off. Maybe, just between me and you, you can tell me what happened, and I'll see something in there. I checked out your sheet. You're in here for the rest of your life anyway, so what's it to you?"

"What the fuck are you talking about?" There it was, the F-word.

"This goes way back, but I doubt murder is ever forgotten. That guy who lived across the street from your brother, that's what I'm talking about."

Sanderson burst into laughter. "God, this is too much. Sure I can help you out. I never killed the guy. I've killed a lot of people since and, yeah, I'll do the rest of my life here."

Taylor didn't know what to believe. "What do you mean you never killed him? The guy's ex gave you quite a ton of money for it. I know that for a fact."

"Oh yeah, I took the money. And I kept my mouth shut 'cause I chickened out."

"So who killed him?"

"Well, I didn't. I had never killed anyone before that, although I'd mouthed off about it quite a bit. I often claimed to be owed a bunch of money for just having killed someone to try to get money loaned to me. Guess what, it never worked. When that lady offered me a bunch of money to kill her ex, I figured it be easy money."

"But the guy's dead, right?" Taylor asked. His heart was pounding and he felt like he was still pulling this off.

"I don't know. The insurance company paid the lady off and she paid me off." He paused for a moment. "Look, you know I'm going to deny all this if it comes up later."

"It won't. It's not like I'm going to get this guy off by coming up with a lifer to take the rap for him. I'm just looking for something that can point away from him."

"I had the guy in the trunk of his own car, heading up north into the mountains near Mount Baker." Sanderson seemed to enjoy telling the story. "I'm going down this back road, trying to get up the nerve to pull over and do it. The guy opens the trunk from the inside, leaps out when I'm going fifty miles an hour, and rolls off the road, God knows where. He looked like a little rag doll. I pulled the car over and took off after him. He rolled down this huge embankment and was looking up at me from about one hundred feet away. He had this real blank look on his face. I'll never forget that as long as I live—it really creeped me out. He didn't look afraid, he looked lost. Before I knew what to do, he took off. Ran like a jackrabbit. He had such a head start, and there was no way I'd catch him, so I just got back in the car and took off.

"On the way back, I picked up a hitchhiker. I was going to rob him. I did that a lot. Pick someone up, rob them, and then just leave them at the side of the road. But I picked the wrong guy to mess with. He looked real meek and mild. Those are the ones I always picked. He's in the car for ten seconds and he's got a gun in my face. I actually pissed my pants I was so scared. He got quite a

kick out of that. But I did a good on one on him. I was
flying down some back road and jammed the car into
park. He didn't have his seat belt on and was taken totally by surprise. His head hit the dashboard so hard I think
it busted about every bone in his face. I thought he was
dead. I got out of the car to try to figure out what to do. I
was going to just leave the car there and take off. I must
have trashed the transmission when I locked it up. I'm
sitting on the edge of this cliff overlooking the ocean and
the car is rolling towards me. It damn near ran me over. I
jumped out of its way and it rolled right off a cliff and
smashed down on these rocks about a hundred feet
below.

"I had just started to take off when I realized that my
backpack was in the car. It had a lot of stuff with my name
on it. There was a path down to the car and I hiked down.
I got my pack out of the car. If the guy wasn't dead from
his head smashing against the dashboard before, he was
most definitely dead now. His head was pulverized; it
made me puke. Anyway, there was gas all over. For some
reason, I'm not sure why, I lit the car up. It exploded and
practically killed me. That was a pretty dumb thing to do
in terms of attracting attention. But the car was pretty
well-hidden so there wasn't anyone who saw it. I was able
to hike back up and walked all the way back to the highway without a single car passing me. It took me all day. I
called one of my buddies from the highway and he came
and picked me up."

Taylor couldn't figure out why this guy would make
up such a preposterous story.

"So what happened to the first guy, the one you kidnapped?" Taylor asked.

"I didn't think he ever got a good look at me; I had a
mask on when I got him into the trunk, and when he saw
me without it I was real far away and he must have been

pretty dazed. So I figured I was safe, but that the deal was off. But the lady, she gets a hold of me and says what a great job I'd done. Looked like a total accident. I had no idea what she was talking about. I just figured I had to get the money as fast as possible.

"Anyway, it turns out that the skid made it look like the car went over the edge. And the body was so burned up and crushed that they must have figured it was the owner. They didn't have that DNA crap back in those days. I doubt they looked into it very hard. In real life, everyone goes for the easy answer first. I was real scared at first 'cause she told me I'd have to wait for the insurance to settle. I didn't get the money for about two months and I figured he was going to show up and blow the whole thing. I have no idea what ever happened to the guy. Certainly he would have gone to the cops; I robbed him, took his wallet and everything. I kidnapped him. You, being a private eye, could probably figure it out." The last part was seeped in sarcasm.

Suddenly, there was a tap on Taylor's shoulder. "Thirty minutes is up," the guard said. "Finish up."

"That might help me out," Taylor said.

"How?"

"I'm not sure; I guess it doesn't really help."

Sanderson gave Taylor an accusing look. "Private Investigator. Bullshit, kid. You think I'm stupid. I recognize who you are; I'd seen you a dozen times from across the street. You're that guy's kid. Look, I wouldn't have told you jack squat if you really were a PI. I'd hate for you to leave thinking you fooled me.

"I just figured you had a right to know the truth. I guess you can go tell your old lady she isn't the murderer she always thought she was."

He always had the best comeback and almost replied, "I'll leave that to McMullin," but figured he had better leave well enough alone and get out of there. "Thanks, man," was all he said.

Sanderson simply said, "Later," and got up and left. It was just an expression because obviously they would not be seeing each other later.

"Come on, let's go," the guard said to Taylor. He retraced his steps to the car without really any idea of what to do next. He was still in a daze when he got in his car and headed back to Seattle.

## CHAPTER FIVE

# Hiking

The trip back was uneventful. Taylor's mind was lost in a fog the entire way back. Before he knew it, he was crossing the bridge across Lake Washington into Seattle. Looking to the south, he could see Mt. Rainier looming up beyond the end of the lake. He couldn't count the number of times he had hiked on it, usually going through the snow fields covering the Paradise-Stevens glacier to Camp Muir at the 10,000 foot level or along the Sunrise ridges on the other side of the mountain. Muir is where summiteers spend the night before climbing to the top, although "spending the night" isn't too accurate. There is very little sleep; the trip to the summit starts during the wee hours of the morning. Taylor had climbed to the summit three times in his life. It was quite a feeling, to be standing on top of a 14,000 foot peak, watching the sunrise, with the whole world laid out beneath your feet.

He tried desperately, all the way back home from Eastern Washington, to come up with some kind of a plan. What the hell had happened to his dad? He doubted that Jack's brother had made up the story. That much was certain. It matched what his mom had told him. Demented ranting was no longer a possibility. But then what? What happened to his dad? Had he figured out the whole thing and fled for his life? That didn't make sense. He would have gone to the cops. Taylor couldn't even guess whether his dad was dead or alive. The only thing he could decide on was that he wanted to find out. He just didn't know how.

Then he remembered that weird girl, Ging, from the other night. Was she for real? She told him that his dad was alive. Stan was convinced she was legit. Maybe it was all lucky guesses—a lot of lucky guesses. Taylor decided to find her and talk to her some more. She was the first one to put the idea in his head that his dad was alive. Perhaps she'd have more answers. At least he wanted to find her and ask her out. Invite her to Bean's for a free latte. See where that would go.

The incense shop was only a few minutes walk from his apartment. He parked the van and headed directly to the shop. Walking inside, he entered a portal to a different world. There was something for each sense. Clouds of incense drifted all through the store. Peaceful acoustic guitar music was playing, and it sounded like it was coming from all around. A plate of granola treats beside a "Help yourself to what you need" sign was on the counter. Ging was up on a ladder hanging a tapestry from the ceiling, stretching her taut body upwards. Which of his senses was she there to satisfy? Was she for his eyes or his touch? Perhaps a twofer to cover those last two senses. He chucked to himself as he stared at her gorgeous figure, almost perfectly lined up with the "Help yourself to what you need" sign. Life was so full of subtle messages.

She turned and their eyes met.

"Taylor, I figured I'd bump into you," she said. Her voice was so deep and husky. Everything about her was dark except the hint of a smile on her face. Taylor couldn't tell if she was happy to see him.

"Hey, Ging, how's it going? Recover from the other night?" He remembered how much she had drunk. She couldn't have weighed more than one hundred pounds.

"Yeah. Just another night."

"Listen, I was pretty drunk. You said something pretty weird right before you left. What did—"

"Your father," she interrupted him.

"Was that for real?" he asked.

"Look, I shouldn't have said anything. I'm real tired of this freak show life I live. I just want to be normal." She suddenly seemed so sad and tired. "Yes, it's for real. Call it a gift or a curse. I used to think it was such a gift; it has become such a curse. Everyone is so afraid of me."

"So, you think my dad is really alive?"

"You don't understand, Taylor. I know your dad is alive."

"What else do you know?" he asked, a strange feeling taking over his stomach.

"Not much. You see, it's like dreams to me. I just get images, thoughts. It's impossible to describe. I've tried. It comes and goes without warning. It's like living next to someone who plays the TV real loud. I can hear it through the walls, but I can't turn it on or off. I can't decide what channel to watch. I can't even figure out what it is half the time.

"At first, I thought I was going crazy. It started when I was in seventh grade. Sometimes I'd go months, sometimes just days, before it'd happen again. It stopped for a couple of years at one point. When I walked into the bar and saw you, when I looked into your eyes, it hit me, about your dad."

"There's nothing more you can tell me?"

"I can tell you what I saw, if you can really call it seeing. I saw a man; he's your father. I can't explain to you how I know that. He just is. He was walking through snow. Just walking. Not looking for anything, not running away from anything, just walking peacefully. I could feel that: totally at peace." She was beginning to cease talking in sentences. Her speech became stream-of-consciousness. She closed her eyes.

"Peace…he's happy…but alone…deep inside…loneliness…lost memories…he doesn't understand."

Her voice began to crack. She opened her eyes and it looked like she might cry. "He doesn't even know what he lost, just that it is lost." She covered her eyes with her hands and drew in a deep breath. Taylor thought she was going to faint, she looked so exhausted. Ging said nothing for several minutes.

"I'm OK. Do I scare you?" she asked. She'd regained her composure.

"No, not particularly," he answered without even thinking. "I'm heading up to work, you wanna come for some coffee?" he asked. "My treat."

"Sure. Tina's already ten minutes late. I'm supposed to be off. I'll just lock up, she's got keys." Ging pulled out one of those "Be back at" signs with the red hands of a clock. She set it twenty minutes ahead and put it on the door.

"Hopefully, there won't be any incense emergencies," Taylor joked, trying to lighten things up.

Ging laughed. It was a nice laugh. "Thanks for making me laugh. I needed that. You'd be surprised how seriously some people take their incense. Can I admit something to you? Stan was so funny. He came into the store, flirting with me, pretending to be so into incense. I thought it was kind of cute. He must have thought I was a total idiot. I could tell he was a real nice guy so I played along. I never admitted that to him. I know how fragile your male egos are."

"Stan's probably one of the nicest people I've ever met," Taylor added. "He was kind of like an older brother to me. I miss him a lot."

"He'll be back," she said.

They continued talking as they walked up the street to Bean's. It was real normal talk. Taylor didn't really have to go into work; he just wanted to spend more time with Ging.

As soon as he walked in he felt at home, in his place. Two students were at a table in front playing backgammon. He walked behind the counter and made two lattes, grabbed a couple of muffins, and headed with Ging to a table in the back. He was attracted to her, but a voice inside of him was saying that this was, most certainly, one big pack of issues sitting in front of him, despite the packaging.

"So, tell me about your father," she said.

Taylor gave her the short version. Even that was a long story. He included the events of the last couple of days. Certainly, almost the entire story was still true. Everything he had recently learned only changed the ending. Kind of like someone replacing only the last page in a book. The last page can be a pretty important one. She listened intently to the whole thing.

"It must have been very hard for you," she said sympathetically. It sounded real sincere.

"But I don't know what to make of it," Taylor said. "I spent my whole life thinking my dad died in a car crash when I was two. That's what everyone told me. Then my mom tells me she had him killed. Now what? He's alive?"

"I guess it would have been better for you to just think he had been killed, huh?" she said. That was exactly what he was thinking.

"What I can't figure out is, if he really is alive, why wouldn't he have come gotten me? I was living with him. If he knew my mom was behind it, wouldn't he have gone to the cops? What did you say earlier? 'He didn't even know what he had lost.' There is something else: that guy at the prison. I guess he's the last one to have seen my dad. He said my dad was looking up, with this real blank look on his face, this lost look. That's what he said."

"It sounds like he jumped out of the trunk of a moving car and rolled one hundred feet down a hill; I'd be pretty dazed myself," she said.

"That's what I'm thinking. He didn't have any ID on him. Sanderson told me he took his wallet. Maybe he got a concussion and amnesia. That is the only thing I can think of. He wouldn't have even known what he lost, right?" Taylor said, repeating Ging's words right back to her.

"It's possible, I guess. Anything's possible. He would have had to wind up somewhere."

"Walking in the snow," Taylor said philosophically, again repeating back her words.

"Yeah, walking in the snow," she said as she finished her latte. "Man, I need a drink, but I don't want one," she said.

Taylor remembered her guzzling down the drinks the other night: "Just another night," she had said.

"Keep me out of the bar," she pleaded with him. Taylor was surprised by her sudden closeness to him. He felt inexplicably drawn to her.

"Sure." Taylor liked drinking, but there sure was so much more to life. It was starting to get dark outside. He loaded up and launched the Hail Mary: "How about I cook you dinner?" It just came out without thinking. "My place is just down the street. No bar."

"I'd love that," she said. Taylor envisioned the goal line referee signaling for touchdown and the crowd going crazy.

Taylor had no idea what he had at home, so they stopped off at the grocery store on the way there. He almost got a bottle of wine but realized that it'd be better to skip that. He wanted just a normal, nice time. It was real pleasant, moving though the grocery store together. It turned out that they both shopped there. She admitted having seen him there a few times. How could he have missed her?

They bought two bags of groceries and walked the rest of the way to his apartment building, an old three-story brick building one block off of University Avenue.

"My God!" Ging exclaimed when she saw the full array of emergency equipment, lights flashing, outside of Taylor's place. Fire truck. Aid truck. Ambulance. Policeman.

"Trust me, it's nothing," Taylor said. It was his turn to be psychic.

As they got to the top of the stairs, they saw the whole team at the apartment at the end of the hallway, Dale and Sharon's. Dale was rubbing his hands through his hair listening to one of the paramedics. Taylor caught just a glimpse of Sharon, sitting on a couch with an oxygen mask on. She looked scared out of her wits; Dale looked pissed off. Everyone was telling Sharon to just relax, telling her everything was going to be OK. Taylor recognized almost all of the various people attending to her. They were the regulars, just doing their job.

Taylor led Ging into his apartment. The last time he had been there he'd woken up passed-out right inside the floor. He put the groceries on the kitchen table and instinctively opened the refrigerator for a beer. Again, he realized that wouldn't be a good idea. Thinking quickly, he put the vegetables in and closed the door. When he turned around, Ging was staring at him. He was no psychic, but he could read what was in her mind.

There is always that uncomfortable moment before the first kiss. Both of them were thinking the same thing, both were unsure. Their eyes told it all.

"Come here, you," Taylor whispered.

Without taking her eyes off his, Ging glided towards him, her lips drawn to his, like the moment just after the roller coaster crests the hill. He took her in his arms and kissed her, a long passionate kiss. She held him tight in her arms; he moved his hands up to her cheeks and caressed her face as they kissed. Her body pushed up against his, every curve fitting into him. Slowly, her body began rubbing up against him. He continued kissing her, on the lips, along the jaw, down her throat. She moaned quietly as he began exploring her body with his lips and his hands. Time stopped, as clothes slowly began to shed. It was a truly perfect moment, if there was such a thing. It seemed to last forever. Hours later, sometime around midnight, they both cried out as their bodies collapsed into each other. They lay silently, holding each other in a tight embrace, enjoying the afterglow as they both dozed off.

They slept the night together in a deep, peaceful sleep. Taylor awoke with the sun in his eyes. He looked at Ging sleeping in his arms. She looked so content, so beautiful, so sexy. All traces of her inner turmoil were gone. She had a smile on her face as she slept.

She awoke while he was staring at her.

The smile that had been on her face as she slept quickly vanished.

"Good morning," she said. "Some dinner you made." He couldn't tell if she was happy or regretful. She got up and went into the bathroom. Taylor grabbed the box of

Tic Tacs by his bed and filled his mouth, crunching away the morning breath. When she came out, still naked, she took him in her arms and kissed him. She tasted like toothpaste. It was a nice kiss. It left a smile on her face. And his.

They spent the morning together. Taylor made a pot of coffee and cooked a big breakfast. They were starved.

He caught her looking at his CD's.

"Put something on," he said. He had a huge array of music: old stuff, new stuff, a little of everything. She put on the Stones' "Black and Blue."

They ate their breakfast and talked. Various things came up. Music: they both liked a huge range of music and their tastes overlapped a lot. Stan: they both missed him. Seattle: they both had lived in or near the city, Taylor his whole life, Ging since she was two. So much of them seemed to overlap. Ging, like too many people who live in Seattle, had never been into the mountains. Taylor promised to show her some places up there that would blow her mind. The subject of alcohol came up. Ging admitted the obvious, that she kind of had a drinking problem.

"I drink out of boredom, more than anything," she said. "Last night, with you, here, I didn't have the slightest desire for a drink," she said with a smile. "Thanks."

"You're welcome. Say, what are you doing today? I'm not working today. Would you like to go hiking up in the mountains?" It was looking like it was going to be a nice day. He was still riding down the first hill on the roller coaster, still enjoying the first thrill.

"Man, I'd love to. Can we stop by my place first?"

"Sure, but give me a minute to get ready," he said.

She hung out at his place while he showered, cleaned up and got dressed. He packed a backpack with everything they'd need then they walked to her place. It turned out to be real close.

Her place was as feminine as his was masculine. Where he had candles stuck into wicker covered Chianti bottles, she had elaborate arrays of candelabra. Where he had his CD's scattered randomly in several shoeboxes, she had a finely carved, wooden CD shelf. Where he had posters of rock bands and outdoor scenes haphazardly plastered on the walls, she had framed lithographs. He recognized most of them from the art history class he had taken at The U. Her apartment was filled with the sweet smell of wonderful incense.

He lay down on her couch while she showered and got ready. He toyed with the idea of climbing in the shower with her but decided not to. He liked hiking in the mountains almost as much as sex. He didn't want to miss the hike, there'd be time for sex later, he knew. It wasn't long till she was all ready.

They walked to his van and headed east out of the city, towards the mountains. The same drive he had made just two days ago to Walla Walla and, in reverse, just yesterday. The Cascade Mountains are less than an hour east of Seattle. They would cross Lake Washington, pass through the suburbs on the east side of the lake, and then head up through foothills into the mountains.

It was just after noon when they reached the trailhead. He had chosen a hike to Mulakua Lake, just west of the mountain pass. It didn't involve the massive climbing that most of the hikes in the mountains required, but its destination was amongst the most beautiful he had ever seen. An alpine lake nestled amongst sheer cliffs. The other thing he liked about the hike is that the terrain would change several times along the way, giving her a good sample of what the Cascades had to offer. The trail followed a series of long valleys, walled on either side by steep cliffs rising at least a thousand feet up. The terrain was a slow rise to the end of each valley, where there would be a short climb into the next.

Ging turned out to be in pretty good shape. She had told him she was a runner. That explained the firm, fit body. She had no problem with the hike. They went first along a winding trail through a dense evergreen forest, climbing slowly. Then they came out in an open field, about a half-mile wide, bordered on both sides by thousand foot cliffs. One side of this valley was full of enormous boulders, deposited long ago by the glaciers that carved it. They hiked across, the boulders on one side, a steep drop off into a creek on the other side. The trail climbed slowly for a mile or so until it reached the back of the valley, where it climbed steeply with switchbacks. Off to the right, the creek cascaded off a cliff in a glorious waterfall. After they climbed up the back of the valley they took a break and enjoyed the view. They looked down the length of the where they had crossed, the cliffs running along both sides. Ging stood, hands on hips, barely winded.

They took a short break and continued onwards. Cresting the hill, they left the valley behind them. They crossed through another forested area. The trail meandered around following the path of the creek. They crossed the creek and began to head up another hill. They crested this hill and dropped down into the lake basin. Taylor's favorite part of the hike was the lake. It's a high alpine lake, which is to say it's nothing more than snow melt from the winter that gets trapped and doesn't have time to run out. The creek they had been following all along, Denny Creek, runs out of the lake and down into the Snoqualmie River at the bottom, near where they had begun. The lake is bordered on two sides by huge, towering cliffs that meet at the back of the lake. Only one side of the lake is open. It is here that the water runs out a narrow channel.

As soon as Ging saw the lake, she stopped and marveled. She was speechless.

Taylor came up from behind her and put his arms around her. "Gorgeous, isn't it?" he whispered into her ear.

"Man, I can't believe it. I've lived my whole life less than an hour away from here and never seen it. This is so beautiful."

She reached back with her arms and put them behind him. Taylor turned her around so she was facing him and put his arms around her and kissed her. They embraced for a moment, and then both turned towards the lake. There was actually a pair of lakes with a small patch of land between them. They walked along the edge of the first lake, scrambling over the boulders that rimmed it. They hiked along the rear lake and climbed onto a huge boulder that was just at the edge of the lake. It was twice the size of Taylor's van and flat on the top. The midafternoon sun was shining down on them as they napped on the boulder, peacefully. They held each other in their arms. They had the whole lake to themselves.

Taylor didn't know how long he was asleep, but it couldn't have been very long. The sun hadn't moved much in the sky. He looked at Ging, asleep next to him. She awoke under his gaze. The smile that was on her face as she slept didn't vanish this time as she awoke—a good sign.

"This is so peaceful," she said. "Thanks for showing this to me. I'll never forget this moment."

"I know what you mean. Well, we better get going. I'd hate to add getting lost in the dark to your day. You'd probably not forget that either."

The hike down was quick, all downhill. They talked the whole way back to the trailhead. Ging dropped a couple of well-received hints about spending another night together. There was one strange moment where she just stopped and stared off into space. Taylor thought she was catching her breath so he just waited. They had been talking and she stopped in mid-sentence.

"Hey, you OK?" he asked. She didn't answer. After about a minute, she suddenly snapped out of it. She looked lost for a second, then looked at him and blinked her eyes a few times. When her gaze met his, a smile appeared on her face.

"Sorry," was all she said, without any explanation. Things were going so well that Taylor thought he'd best leave it alone. All of a sudden, she seemed fine again. "Come on, slowpoke," she joked as she headed on.

It was getting close to sunset when they reached the parking lot at the trailhead. They did a high-five to mark the end of the hike.

"How about I cook you dinner, at my place this time," she said sarcastically.

"Sounds good to me." He was beginning to feel real comfortable with Ging.

They headed back and parked the van outside his place. They went up to his apartment and he got cleaned up first. He was in the shower about five minutes when she unexpectedly climbed in with him. One advantage of living in an apartment building is an inexhaustible supply of hot water. Taylor discovered that his place, in fact, had at least one hour of hot water. He was grateful for that.

Afterwards, they got dressed and headed to her place. It was almost ten o'clock.

"Kind of late for dinner, I guess. How about we pick up a pizza, my treat," she said. "I owe you."

"Sounds good to me," he said. He was in such a good mood; anything would be fine for him.

They cut over to University Avenue and picked up a pizza to go. It was one of those places, almost extinct, where you can watch the guys hand-toss the dough. It was worth the twenty-minute wait. They talked while their pizza was being made.

"Really, Taylor, thanks for today. I mean it. What an incredible place."

"Sure thing. Would you like to go hiking some other time?" It was an obvious thing to say.

"I'd love to," she said. "I gotta get out more. Stop taking things so seriously. I had the best time today since...I don't know when."

"Me too," he said. It sounded kind of phony but he meant it. "Hey, our pizza's ready," he said as he heard them call her name. She paid for the pizza and picked up a six-pack of soda. They walked along The Ave to her apartment.

"Make yourself at home," she said, putting the pizza on the kitchen table. She went into her bedroom to change.

Taylor looked around. You can tell a lot about someone by looking at their home. Hers was no exception.

Her apartment gave the impression of her incredible depth. One wall of her living room was entirely covered with floor to ceiling bookshelves, obviously homemade but very well crafted. He made his way over to check out the books; she had an immense personal paperback library. All the books looked to be secondhand. Taylor considered himself to be well-read, but suddenly felt like he was in the presence of someone much more so. He scanned the spines; most of the books he considered to have had the most impact on his life were in her collection.

"I read a lot," she said from behind him, startling him. "It helps me feel like I can get away."

"Yeah, I love to read," he said. "But I haven't been doing it as much as I used to."

"Quick, without thinking, what are your favorite five books?" she asked.

He paused, trying to rack up a list in his mind.

"I said no thinking," she said with a smile.

"Well, that's pretty hard to say. I'd have to say *On the Road* by Jack Kerouac, *A Prayer for Owen Meany* by John Irving…anything by Kurt Vonnegut. They all kind of blur together. Can I count that as one?"

"Sure," she responded.

Taylor continued. "Let's see, that's three. OK, how about Tom Robbins, *Even Cowgirls Get the Blues*. And…and let's see. Can I count the whole Hobbit/Lord of the Rings thing as one?"

Ging nodded her head. "I guess so."

"OK, that's five. I can't say they're my favorite five or anything, but certainly five good ones."

She went over to her bookshelf, pulled a bunch of books off, and set them on the table in front of him. They were the four Tolkein books and three others, *On the Road*, *A Prayer for Owen Meany*, and *Even Cowgirls Get the Blues*.

"Hey, what gives, nothing by Vonnegut?"

She walked back over to the shelf. "You didn't say which one." She pulled an armful of books, returned, and dumped them in his lap. "Satisfied?" she said.

They ate the pizza and talked late into the night. Finally, to the surprise of both of them, it began to be light outside.

"Sunrise," she said.

They both stood up and watched the colors dance across the sky as the sun slowly rose. Taylor, for his entire life, would look back on that as the most beautiful sunrise he had ever seen.

Just as the disk of the sun peeked up over the distant hills, Ging and Taylor pulled together, each reading the other's mind. They kissed and kissed as the sun rose. In what seemed like an instant and an eternity at the same time they slipped each other's clothes off. They made love together into the morning hours, finally sinking off to sleep in her bed. Taylor had never felt so comfortable in his whole life.

# CHAPTER SIX

# The PI

Time passed after that for Taylor and Ging in a warm bliss. Ging spent a couple of nights a week with him, sleeping at his place, and he did likewise at hers. They had enough time apart to maintain their lives from before they met, and enough time together to enjoy and explore each other's passions. The time apart seemed to ensure that time together would always be appreciated to its fullest.

For Ging, too, these days were filled with happiness. Gone was the serious expression she had so wrapped herself up in for years, replaced by a frequent smile on her face. There also seemed to be a constant brightness in her dark eyes. She, too, had fallen in love. It would be for the first and last time in her life.

Knowing that Taylor wasn't too comfortable with her psychic gift/curse, Ging avoided the subject all together. She told him her first, and last, lie—that for some unexplained reason it had gone away. Although untrue, it was her deepest wish that she would lose this ability. It served no purpose for her except complicating life and her emotions. Perhaps love chased it off, she said. That seemed to put him at ease. As time went on, this did begin to approach the truth, as her flashes of imagery from dimensions next door became less and less frequent. While before she'd consider herself lucky if even several days passed between them, eventually, as time with Taylor passed on, she'd often go weeks, sometimes even months. She wished it would just go away entirely and leave her with a happy and normal life. She could imagine such a life ahead of her, just out of reach.

Their nights were filled with flaming passion. They both discovered within themselves a strong desire for experimentation, and constantly found new heights of ecstasy with each other. They had their respective day-to-day responsibilities, he at the coffee shop and she at the incense store, and they drifted through the day hours on the vivid memories of the previous nights, together and the anticipation of the nights ahead.

They connected in that rare way that many people never experience. It was far more than love, if there is such a thing. It truly felt to each of them that they were lost souls, long since separated and finally rejoined. Taylor felt so inexplicably drawn towards Ging. He shared this feeling with her and she told him that she felt exactly the same. They didn't ask too many questions about it.

They spent much time together, sharing their experiences and feelings with each other. Taylor took her on many high mountain hikes in the Cascade and Olympic Mountains. On their two-month anniversary, they climbed together to Camp Muir, the day camp at 10,000 feet on Mount Rainier. Tears welled up in Ging's eyes as she stood on top of a boulder pile behind the crude dormitory camp nestled into the rock, gazing at the distant mountain peaks rising up out of the clouds below. Taylor pointed each of them out: Mt. St. Helens and Mt. Adams to the south, Mt. Baker to the north. The top of Mt. St. Helens had been blown off in a volcanic eruption in 1980, leaving it an odd sight, a mountain without a top.

They embraced, two miles high, oblivious to anyone else around them.

Summer turned into fall and the famous Seattle drizzle arrived. Fall was the time of year where Taylor often felt bored. Most of his pastimes revolved around being outdoors. It was a tough time of year for him. Ging introduced him to all sorts of places he'd never been around Seattle. She seemed to know a multitude of interesting places to just hang out and pass the time. He used to do that all the time when he was younger and taking classes. For some reason, as he got older, it had become less frequent. Just as he had shown her so much of the outdoors over the summer, she showed him the indoors in the fall. Once again, they were like two long-lost puzzle pieces fitting perfectly together.

They continued creating the kind of fiery passion that made every night together as exciting and fulfilling as the first. Ging felt so safe sleeping in his arms; Taylor never felt anything as arousing as her naked body held closely against his. They learned every nuance of each other's bodies and desires, exploiting them and unleashing endless pleasures.

The emergency calls kept coming in on schedule, a few times a month, from the apartment at the end of the hallway. At first Ging was upset at Taylor for making fun of the whole thing. After the first couple calls, she began to lighten up about it. They both began to know some of the paramedics on a first name basis.

Taylor thought less and less about the bizarre mystery surrounding his father, having hit what seemed like a dead end. Also, falling in love with Ging had pretty much taken his mind off it. He still had a nagging feeling that he should look into it more, but he didn't have any idea how to do so. He and Ging occasionally talked about it, each throwing out ideas, but nothing really seemed to show any promise. It had come to feel like it would be best to just let it go. He wished that his mother had simply died a few days earlier without telling him about his dad. That would have been far better. He was happy now with his life as it was.

Then one day, shortly after Christmas, Ging came running into Bean's all excited and out of breath. It was just after noon and she had the rest of the day off work. They had planned to meet for dinner, after Taylor got off. He'd lost a bet. Ging and Taylor had begun wagering on the number of days until the next emergency call to the building, an over/under deal. Taylor had picked seven days and over. It seemed like a sure win; Ging took the gamble. With only several hours left until day seven, and with Taylor teasing Ging, sirens fired off in the distance. Taylor began to get nervous as they approached. Finally, the team pulled up to the building and Taylor had to admit defeat as they raced into the building and down the hallway.

He hadn't expected to see her at Bean's for several hours and was pleasantly surprised that she was arriving early; he had just been thinking of her.

"Taylor, I was talking to this new girl we just hired today," she was still out of breath. "And we got talking about things, you know, like where are we are from, et cetera, blah blah blah. Well, it turns out she has a brother that works for a private investigator downtown."

Taylor didn't see why this was such a big deal. He didn't make any connection about what she was talking about and his father. Daydreams of the night before were running through his mind. She had come out of the bathroom dressed in an old T-shirt that came down long enough to just cover her panties. As they embraced and kissed, he pulled off her panties and tugged the T-shirt at the neck and began to hear it tearing. He ripped it right off her body, the sound of its tearing blended in with the sound of her loud erotic moaning…

"Taylor, ARE YOU LISTENING TO ME!!" she shouted, somewhat annoyed.

"Uh, sorry, I was thinking about something," he said meekly, with a childish grin on his face.

"So, I was saying, this girl's brother is an assistant for a PI downtown. He basically spends his day following around husbands or wives and photographing their indiscretions—divorce cases and things like that. Anyway, her brother came in today. He was telling me about his job and I asked him if he could help us with the thing about your dad."

Now Taylor was listening. The thoughts of the night before were filed down in the memory album for later.

"Their business isn't doing too hot. He was sure the PI he works for could help out," she said.

"Really?" he replied. "What exactly could they do?" Ging had his full attention now.

"Brian was pointing out that it is pretty easy to get hospital records. Even from years ago. If your dad was brought in, even as a John Doe, there should be a paper trail, still today. He said he had just looked into something like this last year. The only hard part was that all the records from that long ago are kept in warehouses, and it takes forever to locate the right box—a needle in a haystack."

Taylor didn't really see that this was such a big deal, but Ging seemed so excited about it that he didn't want to hurt her feelings. She sensed his lack of enthusiasm. "Hmmm," he said.

"Don't you see? You could at least prove to yourself that he was alive after the accident." She always wondered if he was skeptical over her telling him his father was alive; this would prove it to him once and for all. "Or prove that he's dead. That'd at least give you a sense of closure. Or, who knows, maybe it'll tell you where he lived. There must have been an address on the release."

"Come on. Let's go see him," she said excitedly. "He said he'd be around all day and we could go down there right now. What could it hurt?"

Taylor still wasn't too enthusiastic about the whole thing, but he figured it'd be fun to hang around downtown with Ging anyway; that was always adventuresome. He'd finished up the weekly paperwork that was the job for the day, so taking off the rest of the day would be no problem. The two guys he had working for him today, Jerry and Bob, were relative old-timers, having been at Bean's for almost two years. They'd be in charge during his absence. Taylor always tried to have one experienced person working at all times so he could take off with little notice. Stan was always so secretive and protective about what he did that he always made a big deal out of not being at the shop, even though he only took off a day or two every month. Looking back on it from the point of now being in charge of the place, it seemed pretty silly to Taylor. Taylor felt no need to make himself indispensable.

"Sure, I'm in," was all Taylor said. He told Jerry that he had to go downtown to take care of something. Jerry gave an exaggerated glance at Ging and said sarcastically to Taylor, "Yeah, Taylor, go downtown." They both laughed at that. Taylor didn't bother trying to convince Jerry that they really were going downtown. He enjoyed the way that everyone seemed to envy him and Ging.

Taylor and Ging waited on University Avenue to catch the number seven metro bus to downtown. In the time it would take to walk home and get his car, not to mention the huge amount of time he'd waste driving around looking around for parking, they could make a dozen bus trips. Taylor was a frequent bus rider when it had to do with getting around Seattle. Every month he bought a pass for unlimited bus riding. It cost as much as just a couple of downtown parking fees. He had turned Ging into a bus rider. They rode all around the city together often.

Within minutes, the number seven came down The Ave. It would go downtown via Capital Hill and pass within a block of where they were headed. They flashed their passes to the driver and took a seat in the middle of the bus.

Seattle buses are always pretty bizarre collections of the city's dwellers. Sitting in front of them was a strange-looking guy with thick glasses mumbling to himself and scrawling notes into a small notebook with a stub of a pencil. Taylor had seen him before and was curious what delusional project was going on in front of him. He crouched up just enough to look over the man's shoulder. The guy was staring out the window, apparently focusing his attention on the parked cars that the bus was passing. Every once in awhile he would mutter to himself "Ah-uh!" and jot something down. Taylor looked at the book. The page he could see was filled with numbers and letters in no apparent organization. Taylor watched him as the bus left the University District, crossing the U bridge and heading up into Capital Hill. The road climbing up Capital Hill seemed to be a gold mine for this fellow; he must have jotted down a dozen entries. Eventually, Taylor figured it out: it was license plate numbers that were being recorded. This guy was obviously off his rocker. Probably harmless, he figured, but probably schizophrenic.

Taylor continued to watch and, suddenly, the man jumped up and turned around and shouted something at Taylor. It sounded like "Nairobi!" but surely he had heard it wrong. The guy had a crazed look in his eyes. The situation had quickly gone from amusing to somewhat scary. The bus driver, as well as everyone else in the bus, was doing his best to pretend that they didn't notice anything out of the ordinary, but obviously they had heard the commotion. A few people stared with fright out of the corners of their eyes, afraid to make eye contact with the situation. Taylor felt Ging clench to his side for protection.

The crazy guy stood frozen, breathing hard, glaring at Taylor. He looked to Taylor like he was frightened out of his wits. Suddenly, without any warning, the man tossed his pencil into the aisle and, as Taylor's attention followed it, dashed off towards the front of the bus, shouting something totally incomprehensible. The driver and the passengers finally began to take notice, or at least were finally forced to admit that they had noticed. The bus driver pulled over for a bus stop and opened the door. The man dove head first out the door, crashing to the sidewalk. Taylor looked at the window and saw him get up, dash across the street, barely miss being hit by a car, and disappear into an alley. Everyone on the bus breathed a simultaneous sigh of relief. The driver seemed only mildly irritated. A frightened, hyperventilating women sitting across from Taylor and Ging pulled a prescription bottle out of her purse and gobbled down a small white tablet. Many people on the bus were now laughing.

With the show over, the bus crossed Capital Hill and then headed down the hill into downtown. They were going to meet Brian and Brian's boss in their Pioneer

Square office. Pioneer Square is the original downtown Seattle. Mostly old brick buildings rebuilt after the famous Seattle fire that burned the city to the ground. In its heart is a dense collection of bars and clubs rivaling Austin's 6th Street or New Orleans's Bourbon Street. On any given night the place resembled a cross between the world's largest bachelor party and a huge frat/sorority bash. Taylor hated this part of the city at night. He preferred the saner and laid back feeling found in an area called Bell Town, where you could go drink and catch a band and not be surrounded by people living their weekend alternate personality. People around Bell Town seemed far more genuine.

They easily found the office. It was in a three-story, an old brick building with a dentist's office, two law firms, two accountants, and the Sterling Private Investigations Company. That sounded pretty professional. It was on the first floor. Taylor and Ging found the office, the door was open. Inside, two people sat at a small table, drinking beer and eating Chinese food out of paper take-out containers. Neither looked the part of a private investigator. One looked to be all of twenty-one, the other was middle-aged and about fifty pounds overweight. He looked like he might have been rugged in his younger years and had let himself go.

"Hey, Brian," Ging said to the younger one.

He looked up, at first without any sense of recognition, then he said, "Oh yeah, hi. I wasn't sure if you were coming down today." He seemed a little drunk. He turned to the older fellow, apparently the Sterling of Sterling PI. "Max, these are the guys I was telling you about," he said excitedly. Max Sterling took a long finishing draw of his beer, trying to look tough, and ended up spilling a good amount of it down his shirt. "Whoopsie," was all he said. It wasn't a good first impression.

Max Sterling held out his hand to Taylor. They shook hands.

"Brian here was telling me about you," Sterling said to Taylor. "We can definitely help you out if you're interested. Missing persons is one of our specialties."

Taylor didn't know what to make of this pair. On one hand, they were drinking at work at noon. That either meant business was so good they could afford to kick back or so bad that it was pointless to wait. He figured it probably was the latter. Brian had pretty much already spilled those beans to Ging earlier.

"I'm definitely interested. What do you think you could do?" Taylor asked.

"Well, for starters, all hospital information is practically public knowledge as long as you know a few people, which I do." He said that with an air of bragging. Taylor could sense the alcohol talking.

"Given some time, we could find the records from the hospitals up in that area and see if your dad was brought in. That leads to where he was discharged. And if we are lucky, that starts a followable trail. We specialize in trail following. It's easy if you know what you're doing."

Max turned to his younger assistant. "Brian here did just that a few months ago, to find a girl that ran away almost ten years ago and hadn't been heard from since. Her dad beat her up and she ran away. We checked the records and it turned out she went to the hospital then took off. We used the hospital records to find out where she went after that. It was a girlfriend's house and the parents still live there today. We did a little flimflamming and got the girlfriend's current address. Then we were able to find the runaway. It's simple stuff if you have the connections." Max was beginning to come across as credible to Taylor.

"She ended up with a good chunk of her father's inheritance, and Brian and I here with a good chunk of the finder's fee." He patted Brian on the back with a sense of fatherly pride. Perhaps business wasn't so bad.

"Give us the word, and we'll look into it for you," Max said as he got up and went to the small refrigerator under the table, pulling out another beer. "Hey, you guys want a Miller?" Max said to Taylor and Ging. Ging's binge drinking had been brought well in control and, after a month or so of cold turkey sobriety, she had returned to a social level of consumption. Taylor had turned out to be an incredibly moderating influence on her. It turned out that she was right when she said she drank out of boredom. As the boredom vanished, so did the excessive drinking.

"Sure," Taylor said without even thinking. Drinking beer with someone went more towards securing mutual trust than anything he could imagine.

"Make it two," Ging added.

"Me too, boss," said Brian. Max gave Brian a questioning look.

They spent the early afternoon drinking beer and mapping out the specifics. Max produced a contract, which Brian instantly proceeded to spill a beer all over. As Brian slumped away to get another contract, Max said to Taylor and Ging, "Don't let the kid fool you, he's great at the job. I taught him everything he knows. So I'll take the credit. He couldn't have found his own feet when he started with me. I'll admit, most of what we do is following people around. It isn't anything like on TV—nothing glamorous. But it pays the bills. Brian does most of the legwork and I provide the direction and the contacts. I was a detective with the Seattle Police for ten years."

Brian returned with the fresh paperwork as Max continued. "My partner and best friend was killed in the line of duty with a bullet that missed my head by inches. I took that as a sign from above. He had no family and listed me as his insurance beneficiary. I used it to set up this business. Hired Brian last year so I wouldn't have to spend so much time on the streets. It's going OK, but I'll admit that we are really beating the bushes for business." Taylor got the impression that this story was always told, unchanged, to new clients—a little history. It seemed rehearsed.

Brian gave the paperwork to Max. Max continued, "But as you would guess, this isn't for free. And we don't do contingency stuff. I figure five hours is what it will take Brian to finish the initial search of records. And it is…" he paused "…a hundred bucks an hour. So, five hundred up front." Max gave Taylor a look that seemed to say that he was waiting for Taylor to barter.

"Fine," was all Taylor said, much to Max's surprise. These guys seemed like a pretty interesting pair. Taylor hadn't given it much thought, but he did realize that he had control over the trust fund now that his mother was gone. It was far more money, many times over, than he needed. He was real happy with his life, as it was now, and had a sinking suspicion that he had to be careful not to let money ruin it. Taylor had continued using the interest to live on and left the principal alone. He was vague with Ging about the source of this extra income. The truth was, he could withdraw five hundred dollars thousands of times over before he'd have to worry. Five hundred dollars didn't seem like much.

Max produced a contract that didn't make too much sense to Taylor. It seemed mainly to protect Max from being held accountable for anything that he or Brian did in Taylor's name. Taylor signed it, under the advice from Max that it was all normal stuff, nothing to worry about, and wrote out a check for five hundred dollars. Taylor trusted him; they'd drunk beer together. He asked them to not cash it for a few days to give him time to move money from a savings account into his checking account. Max agreed to that and said he'd call when either the five hours were used up or when they finished the initial search. He told them it would be a week or so.

They had another round of beers, the deal closer, then Taylor and Ging got up to leave. She had been totally silent during the whole meeting. Taylor couldn't help notice that Brian kept staring at her, checking her out.

They left the office together and were blinded by the late afternoon sun, a rare appearance for late December in Seattle.

"Man, thanks Ging. I'd pretty much resigned myself that there was no way I'd find out any more about the whole thing with my dad," he said, giving credit where credit was due.

Ging put her arms around him and pulled him towards her, giving him a passionate kiss. "You owe me one." They both suddenly wished they were at one of their apartments, together, alone.

They walked hand in hand around the Pioneer Square area, ducking in and out of the various art galleries that ring an area called Occidental Park. They both floated on a combination of beer buzz and togetherness. Ging bought a T-shirt with a Yin-Yang and a couple of postcards. Taylor offered to pay for the shirt as a replacement for the one he had torn off the night before. Ging gave him a naughty grin and said, "If you pay for this one, you'd just tear it off too. And I like this one."

Taylor puffed up his chest and said, "Look, I'll tear off any shirt that I damn well please." They laughed at that together. Ging decided that moment, no matter what, the next time they were alone she was going to rip his shirt to shreds.

They caught the bus home and stopped off at the Italian restaurant a few doors down from Bean's for Taylor to make good on his betting loss.

## CHAPTER SEVEN

# The Dream

He had the dream again, same as before: a faceless man wandering. The face could never be made out—always foggy, misty. Out of the corner of his eye it was always on the verge of getting clearer, but when he turned towards it—blurry. Forgotten memories, almost remembered, blown out like a candle when he got too close. Everything was always clearer at the edge. Blurry when he turned to face towards it.

He looked up and saw a snow-covered mountain, a huge mountain. It was Mount Baker in northern Washington State; somehow he knew that. He was walking all around through wooded trails along the base of the mountain—walking through fog-shrouded trails. Then he was on top of the mountain, looking down from the summit. He popped on a pair of skis and skied down to the bottom, through terrain beyond what a human would ever ski, but it didn't matter. It was a dream. He jumped off huge rocks and flew though the air. He used the skis like wings and a rudder, steering all over the treetops.

Then back at the bottom. Walking in the woods again, the mountain looming above. Searching. Just ahead, in the fog, he could see someone. He knew that this one had answers to questions he had. He tried to run, to catch up. He could hear a voice. All garbled. His feet were like lead, he could barely move. It was like walking in molasses. He fell to the ground and crawled on all fours—that seemed to work better. But however fast he went, he could never catch up. He was running like a monkey on all fours, making pretty good time.

The trail was winding up a steep hill. He rose up on two legs and began running, no longer impeded. He was racing up the hill, whipping around corners. Suddenly he came around a corner and was paralyzed. For a brief moment, he clearly saw a figure standing in front of him that he recognized, and then suddenly everything was all at once clear, but too intense. All senses overloaded. Light so bright it seemed to be coming from the inside of his eyelids. He pressed his hands over his eyes, which didn't help. But it wasn't just his sight. The sound of a million people shouting together burned in his ears. His whole brain was boiling…

Two hundred miles apart, two men jolted awake from the same dream, like diving into freezing cold water. One was alone, in a cabin. He stood up out of bed and stared out his window, tears in his eyes. Looking at the snow-peaked mountain, he wished for one thing. Just to remember his real name.

The other rolled over and put his arms around his lover.


"Taylor, man are you OK?" she asked. "You were yelling."

"Sorry, Ging, I just had a pretty freaky dream." He often said this to her. What he hadn't told her was that it was often the same dream. Like always, it faded so quickly that within moments it was totally forgotten. He just brushed it off. He gave her a kiss on the cheek. "How did you sleep?" he asked, changing the subject.

"Pretty good," she replied, thinking back to what seemed like endless hours of lovemaking the night before.

They looked into each other's eyes; he rolled over on top of her. Suddenly, the phone rang.

"Hold that thought," Taylor said.

He got out of bed, naked, and walked to get the phone. He wagged his naked butt at her as he crossed the bedroom floor. For added comic relief, he gave his butt cheek a hard slap.

"Hello," he said into the receiver.

"Hey, Taylor?"

"Yeah," he replied.

"This is Brian. I have some info for you."

Brian? Taylor quickly racked his brain. He had no idea who he was talking to. "Who is this?" he asked.

"You know, Brian. From Sterling Investigators. We talked last month about your father, remember?"

Taylor's heart skipped a beat. He had pretty much put the whole thing out of mind. It seemed like a dead end. He had wondered why he hadn't heard from them. The thought did cross his mind that they just cashed his check and did nothing. "Oh yeah, what have you found out?" he asked with just a hint of excitement.

"Well, first off, I checked all the Bellingham area hospitals for John Does brought in on the date you gave me. Whatcom County General had one, fits the exact description you gave me. Also, get this: he came in all banged up, and had amnesia. He was in guarded condition, then suddenly a day later was discharged."

"Really?" Taylor asked.

"Really. But that doesn't make sense. He was under police guard. I found his file and there were all sorts of notes about suspicious stuff he said. It didn't make any sense but they figured he was either involved in, or a victim of, a crime and they called the cops right away. I got the names of all the nurses on duty and managed to find one of them, retired but still living in Bellingham. I didn't expect her to remember much about it, it was over twenty-five years ago."

"So did she remember him?"

"She sure did. Quite a memory, this lady. I barely could shut her up. She said that the cop guarding him kept taking off and leaving various nurses to guard the door. They were too busy to really watch. Sounds like the cop did that a lot to the nurses. That really pissed the nurses off. At some point, this guy they were supposed to be watching just walked off. It sounds like both the cop and the nurses were pretty afraid of anyone asking any questions. The nurses would be in deep weeds for not saying anything about the cop not being around, and the cop, he'd have his ass in a sling if they found out he was guarding in absentia, so to speak. So they just put him down as discharged; no one asked any questions. Sounds like so many doctors are involved that everyone figured someone else had handled it."

"Then what?" Taylor asked.

"Well, that's about it, guy. I scoured the Bellingham newspapers about anything relevant, like some guy found wandering around Main Street...but nothing. Sometimes that is how it is. The best I can do, Taylor, is tell you that your dad was in fact alive at that point. The hospital records say most of his injuries weren't too bad: a broken rib, scrapes and bruises. The address on the release form appears to be a phony."

"So, can you look into this further?"

"Look, I'd just be wasting your money. I can't think of anything more I could look into. That was twenty-five years ago. He might have died by now. If he is alive, he doesn't want to be found. Or doesn't remember who he was. The records said he came in with amnesia."

"I got it," Taylor said. "Thanks for finding all that out."

Brian could sense the disappointment in his voice. "Sorry, man. I wish I had more to give you."

"I know. I appreciate it. Bye," Taylor said, hanging up the phone.

"So what's up?" Ging asked. She heard Taylor say Brian's name. Ging was much better with names than Taylor. "Was that about your dad?"

Taylor filled her in on what he had been told. "I just need some sense of closure. It is time to move on. This was real interesting at first, now it is just haunting. I'm ready to let it go. Hell, I was ready to let it go already, before going to the PI"

He saw the hurt look on Ging's face. It was her idea of going to Sterling Investigators, and she was so excited about helping.

"Sorry, I didn't mean that the way it sounded," Taylor said apologetically. "I appreciate your help. It was worth the try."

"Closure, that is a good idea," she said. "It'd do you good to let go of it. Do you think you can just let it go?"

Taylor thought for a moment.

"I think I'm going to cruise up to Bellingham, look at the room in the hospital he was in. Leave it at that. It was the last place he was known to be. Kind of like visiting his gravesite, without knowing if he has one or not."

"You want company?" Ging asked.

"No, I'd rather go alone," he replied. "You under-stand that, don't you?"

"Sure." She sounded somewhat disappointed at being left out, but she understood.

***

It was Sunday. Taylor had the day off and could take most the week off without any problems. First he called Brian back and got the room number that his dad had been in. Then he called Bean's and Roger answered the phone. Roger was the nearest thing Taylor had to a protégé. Taylor had Roger supervising the weekend, and handling much of the orders. That was going real smoothly. Roger would be working until Thursday and could easily run the show while Taylor was gone. He told Roger that something had come up and he'd be gone until Friday. Roger assured him things would be fine. He hung up the phone and had the sudden urge to leave right away.

He grabbed a change of clothes and stuffed them in a backpack. Tunes—he'd need tunes. He grabbed a few CD's: the Grateful Dead's Reckoning, a Stevie Ray Vaughn live CD, and the Rolling Stones' Let it Bleed; It reminded him of the night he met Ging.

He gave Ging a hug and a kiss at the door.

"This is it, closure," he said, kind of sarcastically. He sensed that she was a little unhappy with being excluded but he pretended to not notice this.

"You hurry back, cowboy. And here, if it gets too serious, a friend of mine was listening to this the other day in the back of the shop and it really cracked me up, so I borrowed it." She handed him a "Weird Al" Yankovic CD, Running with Scissors. "Trust me, it'll make you laugh."

He took the CD and his backpack and headed out. In the hallway he bumped into a pair of paramedics. They seemed somewhat confused and unsure of where they were headed. "Down the end of the hallway," Taylor said, and they sprinted off.

He loaded up the VW van, the "habitat" as Stan used to call it. It was always full of miscellaneous junk—enough to live off of for a week, and plenty of reading material to keep him busy, Stan would always say. Taylor told everyone that it was his way of making sure no one would break into it. He was under the impression that no one would break into a messy car. The truth was, though, that he was just a slob.

With the opening licks of Stevie Ray Vaughn, Taylor merged onto I-5 northbound. The Sunday traffic was almost non-existent. In no time, he was cruising through North Seattle and heading into Everett. He wasn't really sure what he was doing but he figured he'd just kind of see where it would lead. Brian, the PI, had given him copies of all the reports, so Taylor had the hospital address as well as the room number. He'd been to Bellingham a couple of times and was pretty sure where the hospital was. Hospitals are pretty easy to find. Just follow the big blue H sign.

He flew through Everett without any delay. Everett is the last bit of Seattle before the Canadian border. There was a time when Everett was a totally separate city, with no man's land separating it from Seattle. But as Seattle grew north, and one-hour commutes became considered reasonable, the two cities kind of merged together. Taylor had a few friends from Everett that would swear that wasn't the case, but that is how it seemed to him. To the north, though, little had changed in decades. As "Voodoo Chile" pounded out of the speakers in his van, Taylor left Everett behind and entered the open road to Bellingham. He passed a road sign telling him that he had sixty miles to go; that didn't seem like much.

It was a pretty uneventful trip the rest of the way. He stopped at a rest stop with free coffee—watered down coffee—and a stale cookie for his donation of a few quarters. That didn't seem free. He assumed it was going to a good cause. He got a second cup of coffee, which they insisted on filling flush to the top. As he walked back to his van, it spilled all over his hand. He was relieved to notice that it wasn't too hot.

There was a carload of college-age kids piling out of an old Dodge Dart. They were all cracking up and reeked of pot. They saw Taylor getting into his VW van with a Dead sticker on the back and looked at him like he was one of their gang.

"Hey dude," one of them said, a tall blond kid with a frat T-shirt on.

"How's it goin'?" Taylor replied, trying to be polite. He didn't really feel like engaging them in any conversation. They seemed pretty wasted, reminding him a little too much of himself at that age. How different it looked now from the perspective of an adult. "Heading north or south?" he asked.

"Heading back to Seattle. Coming back from a road trip to Vacouver."

A second kid, leaning against the Dart and sporting a huge smile and glazed over eyes shouted, to no one in particular, "It's back to be good."

Everyone seemed to understand his dyslexic phrase and it wasn't until about a minute later that the blond kid asked, "What the hell did you say?" They all laughed, Taylor included.

Itching to go, Taylor couldn't think of anything to add so he just said, "Hey, you guys take care," got in his van and drove off. In the rearview mirror, he saw the "Back to be good" kid stumble across the road towards the bathroom. The rest of his group looked to be cheering him on. Taylor wondered if he'd been that silly at that age, knowing the answer.

He got back on the freeway with just about twenty-five miles to go. It was time for a new CD. He popped in the CD Ging gave him, and had one continuous laugh on the way up as "Wierd Al" parodied all sorts of songs. The first one was American Pie, but about was all about Anakin Skywalker and Star Wars: Episode One. It cracked him up.

Before he knew it, he was at the Bellingham exits. He took the downtown exit and it brought him almost immediately to the hospital. He didn't feel ready and talked himself into getting something to eat first. Across the street from the hospital was a hippy-looking coffee shop/restaurant. It was called Gallaria Expresso. It reminded him a lot of Bean's. He went inside and ordered an Americano and a whole-grain waffle. The girl behind the counter looked real familiar but he couldn't place her. He sat down with his coffee and waited for the waffle. The hospital was visible through a big plate glass front window. Taylor sipped his coffee; it was molten hot. He stared at the hospital, expecting some kind of vision or guidance. All that came was a waffle, but a good one. The waffle was delicious, and he hadn't realized how hungry he was until he took his first bite. In no time the waffle was gone and the coffee had cooled off enough to drink. He nursed the coffee, trying to put off leaving and heading across the street to the hospital.

The coffee shop had a nice feel to it, very much like Bean's. Groups of students were scattered around at large tables, conversing. There were two longhaired hippy-types playing Chinese checkers with what looked like a thirty-year-old set. A well-dressed, wealthy looking middle-aged couple was sharing a table with a Goth girl. Probably mom and dad, visiting the daughter they were putting through college.

One of the walls was set up as a mini art gallery. Several different artists were being featured. It all looked pretty interesting. One set was real rainbowy with images of whales and dolphins. Another depicted what looked to be three people, two of them in color and one dark and dreary. It looked to be an adult and a child in color with another adult in black and white. Taylor found that one intriguing but didn't know what to make of it. There was also a set of paintings of dragons. He didn't really like those.

The other walls were peppered with posters: posters advertising bands, posters advertising seminars—even a poster advertising snowshoeing around Mt. Baker. That one caught Taylor's eye. He'd wanted to do that for a long time. Some friend of his had done it last year at Mt. Rainier and told him it was a blast.

The girl who served him his Americano was now cleaning off some tables, and she seemed to keep looking at him. She worked her way over towards his table then smiled at him.

"Taylor, right?" she asked. "I used to work down at Bean's. Remember? Vicki. You were kind of new. I think I left a few months after you got there."

"Yeah, I remember you. How's things with you, Vicki?"

"Pretty good. I'm taking classes at Western, making coffee. It's pretty cool up here. I love it. How about you? Still working at Bean's?"

"I'm a settler," he said. "Actually, I'm managing the place."

"Managing? What happened to Stan? I thought he'd die there." She paused for a second and got real serious. "He's not dead, is he?"

"No. He did kind of wig out and just took off. He hooked up with some Deadheads and caught the last tour. I haven't heard from him since. I hope he's OK."

Vicki told him she had a break coming and made herself a Chai Latte. They talked awhile. She told him a lot of funny stories about Stan. Some he had heard already, but it was good to reminisce. Taylor filled her in on many changes along University Avenue, where the coffee shop was. It was in a constant state of flux, just like the population hanging around, fully turning over every four years. She was surprised to hear that the little organic fruit shop was now a club where bands played. She asked him what he was doing up in Bellingham. He really didn't want to go into it so he lied and said he was on his way up to Vancouver to visit an old friend.

Break time came to an end. Vicki told him she had to go back to work. She asked him to say hi to a few people she knew that were still working at Bean's. They'd talked for nearly an hour. Some break.


Taylor gazed outside the plate glass window of the coffee shop. The hospital was perfectly framed in it. Talking with Vicki had driven the real reason for his visit to Bellingham out of his mind. He had a sudden sense of mixed excitement and dread as he got up to leave.

"Take care, Taylor," Vicki called from behind the counter, her voice almost obscured by the loud sound of milk being steamed.

"Thanks, see you later," he replied as he headed out the door. He often said that to people, even if it was doubtless he'd ever see them again. He always figured that when he was saying goodbye, eventually, he'd run into the person again.

He crossed the street and headed into the main lobby of the hospital. It was the first time he had been in a hospital since his mother died. It had that surreal feeling of emotions off both ends of the scale. People were here both dying and being born—great sadness and joys, optimism and acceptance. The lobby was brightly lit and it hurt his eyes. He put his hands over his eyes for a moment, shielding them. Hospital lobby music drifted into his ears. He stood there, taking it all in.

Taylor took a deep breath and headed to the information counter. There was a visiting hours sign hanging on the wall, and he noticed he was lucky enough to be there during visiting hours. It hadn't occurred to him to check.

There was a large older woman talking to a young pretty girl behind the counter. The older woman seemed highly agitated. There seemed to be some problem related to a hospital bill. The young girl repeatedly told her that she'd have to contact her insurance company; the old woman kept saying that the insurance company told her she'd have to contact the hospital. They volleyed their positions back and forth like tennis players until, finally, the older woman snapped. She yelled what sounded like "King of Prussia!" at the top of her lungs, turned, and stormed out. The girl behind the counter looked frazzled. Taylor noticed a nametag that said she was a volunteer from a local high school. Her name was Shawna.

"Yikes," Taylor said in an attempt to break the tension. He pulled out the slip of paper that he had written the room number on, even though he had it committed to memory. "Hi, Shawna. I'll be a lot easier than her. Can you tell me how to get to room 6231?"

She began to give him a long, detailed set of directions that began with heading down the hallway to the left. Pretty quickly it overwhelmed him and he was too embarrassed to tell her. So he thanked her and headed down the hallway. There was a sign pointing to an elevator and rooms 6000 to 7000. It turned out 6231 was in wing six, floor two, room twenty-one. Simple enough.

The elevator opened up, full of people. Taylor stood back as the elevator emptied. He got in the elevator, by himself, and pushed number two. The elevator opened up and he walked out onto the second floor. A sign in front of the elevator had arrows pointing left for rooms 6200 to 6220, and right for 6221 to 6240. He turned right and headed down the hall. Room 6231 was halfway down on the right. The door was open. He peeked inside...the room was empty. It looked like every hospital room in every hospital in the universe: a pair of beds, wheeled tables at the foot of each, a curtain that could be pulled around the beds, a TV high up on the wall.

Taylor stood between the beds and closed his eyes. He tried to conjure up some feeling of inner peace and the closure he thought he'd, get but all that came to him was a reminder that he had been saying all winter that he wanted to snowshoe up around Mt. Baker near Bellingham. Nothing really came to him except that he suddenly felt kind of foolish. A couple of days off work were a nice break, and the road trip to Bellingham and back would be good for him. So he didn't feel like it was a waste, but coming by the hospital suddenly seemed like a dumb idea. He rationalized that it had been a good excuse to get him to take a few days to himself, which had been a good idea. Sometimes that is just the way things work.

He turned to head out and a nurse with some clipboards bumped into him at the door.

"Can I help you?" she asked.

"No, that's OK," he replied. "I was just looking for someone who was in here. They must have been discharged."

She gave him a strange look, and then passed him at the doorway on her way in.

Taylor retraced his steps and on the way down the elevator made up his mind to spend the next day snowshoeing. Mt. Baker was only an hour or so east of Bellingham. He could spend the day hanging around Bellingham, get a hotel room, and be off in the morning. He popped by the Gallaria Expresso to look at the flyer on the wall. Vicki saw him copying the information off the flyer.

"Hey, you're back. Going snowshoeing?"

"Yeah, I'm gonna give it a try. I love to hike and ski and snowboard. It seems like a combination of the two."

"I've done it a couple of times since moving up here. It's pretty cool. I have a friend that did that one a few weeks ago," she said, pointing to the flyer that Taylor had been copying from. "The guide is a real trip, some mysterious mountain man—a real nice guy. I hear it's great. You'll love it."

"All righty then. Well, goodbye again, Vicki," he said, heading out the door for the second time that day. "Wish me luck."

## CHAPTER EIGHT

# Mountain Man

Taylor drove back out towards the freeway, where he remembered passing a Best Western along a strip of road with some restaurants and fast food joints. He checked in at the hotel, got the room key, and headed back out without even going up to the room. Across the street was a 7-11 where he got a six-pack of Beck's and two of those forty-nine cent hot dogs. "A six-pack of Jeff Beck," the clerk said as he rang up the beer. Dinner and beverage in hand, Taylor headed back to the hotel and went to his room.

It felt good to be alone—alone with his thoughts. If this was closure, it certainly didn't feel like it. For certain, his mother had died mistakenly thinking she had been a murderer. That was troubling. For certain, Taylor had spent his whole life thinking his father was dead, which he wasn't. He had hoped that he could package it and put it all behind him with the visit to the hospital. This wasn't turning out to be the case. It was still so much on his mind.

He finished off the first hot dog and opened a beer. He drank it down; it tasted good. Almost instantly, his nerves began to calm, and he felt relaxed. His mind started shifting to snowshoeing. He called the desk and asked for a 6 a.m. wake-up call and opened a second beer. Pretty

quickly, he found himself nodding off. He let sleep over-
come him without a struggle. His sleep was sound and
deep without any dreams.

Taylor awoke at five-thirty to a gorgeous February sunrise. Having fallen asleep so early, he hadn't needed a
wake-up call. He called the desk and told them he was
awake, showered, and went down to the dining room to
eat breakfast. Snowshoeing, he figured, would be a long
day, so he ate a hearty bacon and eggs breakfast. He
checked out and headed towards Mount Baker on U.S.
20, the Mount Baker Highway.

The flyer had said to meet "Mountain Mike" in the
lower parking lot of the Mount Baker ski area at eight.
That was easy enough. The Mount Baker Highway
winds up into the North Cascade Mountains through a
tiny town called Glacier, then ends at the ski area. He listened to the "Weird Al" CD again as he drove up into the
mountains. There was a long song about hating sauer-
kraut that made him laugh.

In the first parking lot, Taylor saw a van with
"Mountain Mike" painted on the side. Beside the van
stood a large, outdoorsy guy best described as a mountain
man—a mountain man in the rugged, healthy sense, not
the Unabomber way. He looked like one of those guys
that was probably in his late fifties but was in better shape
than people young enough to be his kids. He was about
6' 5" with gray hair cut short. Even with a parka and snow
pants on, it was obvious he was in great shape. It showed
in his face and the health of his skin.

Taylor felt like Mountain Mike reminded him of
someone he'd known before. He couldn't place where or
when. He figured it was probably from Bean's. That happened a lot, with so many people passing through. He

had lost count of how many times he had run into someone who had been a regular years ago, then had just suddenly stopped coming in. People move on, usually never to be seen again.

He pulled up to the van and parked the VW. He got out and introduced himself. "Hi. I'm here for the snowshoeing, you must be Mountain Mike."

If Mountain Mike recognized Taylor, he didn't let on. "Pleased to meet you. I'm waiting on a few more people then we can head out. My name is Mike." He held out his hand and gave Taylor a firm handshake.

"Taylor," he replied.

"Have you ever snowshoed before?" Mike asked.

"No. But I hike all the time. I've always wanted to snowshoe."

"There's not much to it. You just have to know where it is safe to go. Stay away from the avalanche areas. That's where I come in. I know this area like the back of my hand. I'll take you in."

Just then, a beat up white Geo Prizm drove up and parked. A young couple got out with snowshoes and gear. Apparently, the passenger door could not be opened from the inside. First the window was rolled down, then the girl stuck her arm out of the car and opened the door using the outside handle. There was also something wrong with the window, as there was an elaborate procedure for rolling the window back up that required her to guide the window with one hand while turning the knob with the other. She looked very irritated with the guy getting out of the driver side, but this but it passed quickly. This didn't appear to be a new problem.

"All right, here's Chris and Mark," Mike said to Taylor. "Hey guy's, how's it going? We got someone joining us," he said to them. "Taylor, meet Chris and Mark, my regulars. Chris and Mark, meet Taylor." Chris was a short girl in her early thirties who looked part Asian. Mark looked to be about the same age. Both looked like they were in real good shape, and friendly. They all made small talk for a few minutes while Mike headed over to the van.

Mike started unpacking the gear out of his van: a set of snowshoes forTaylor and himself, backpacks, all sorts of gear that Taylor recognized for avalanche survival, shovels, walkie-talkies, and flashing beacons for everyone to wear. Mike saw Taylor staring at the beacons.

"Just a precaution," Mike said. "I know what I'm doing, but you can never be too safe." He gave a flashing beacon to everyone to wear on their jacket. "There's a switch on the side. This will never happen, but if you get in an avalanche, flip the switch and it'll beep and flash a light, and that's how you can be found and dug out."

Taylor couldn't shake the feeling that he knew Mike from somewhere. He also didn't like the sound of the shovels, beacon, and walkie-talkies, but he was aware of the importance of being prepared so it didn't scare him.

Chris and Mark were getting their gear out of the Prizm. The trunk appeared to be held shut with a bungee cord that connected down below the bumper. It looked to be Mark's duty to deal with this.

"All right, let's go," Mike called out. They carried all the gear to the edge of the parking lot where there was a large snow bank. Chris and Mark strapped on their snowshoes while Mike showed Taylor how to put them on. It was pretty straightforward. Mike passed out to everyone a backpack with a shovel and ice ax in it. Taylor put his water bottles and some trail bars into it.

The group climbed onto the snow bank and started shoeing along the trail. They followed prints in the snow that looked fairly fresh. The trail followed a ridge with a view of Mount Baker to the right then dropped down into a valley. The going was slow, much slower than hiking, and a lot more work. They walked on top of the snow along the floor of the valley. Mount Baker was now blocked behind the ridge they had dropped down from. Mike walked alone up front, Mark and Chris were together behind him, and Taylor was alone at the back. It was so incredibly peaceful—everything covered with snow, the sun blazing in a blue sky, the air so cold and crisp. The only sound was the sound of the shoes on the snow. They crossed along the open valley and began climbing a long hill at the back. It looked like it went on forever. Whenever they got to what looked like the top, it was just a false crest with more beyond it. Taylor seemed to have unlimited energy. Outdoors always did that to him.

Everyone kept to themselves, even Mark and Chris. They shoed near each other but didn't talk at all. It was good for Taylor, so relaxing. He wasn't much in the mood for company, and it seemed the rest were the same.

Finally they came to the top of the ridge that formed the back of the valley. "Let's take a break," Mike said, taking off his pack and putting it down. Taylor turned around and looked down into the valley that they had just crossed. It was immense and wide, far larger than anything he had seen in the Central Cascades along I-90 where he normally hiked. The North Cascades have a reputation for that. He could see the trail of their prints, and in the far distance, a small set of dots just coming down the far ridge into the valley.

Mark and Chris were making snow angels atop a huge drift off to the side. Taylor lay flat on his back on top of some snow and rested. Mike seemed lost in his thoughts.

Taylor drifted off for a moment, half-asleep in a dream. He was a little kid again. Someone was pushing

him around in a little tyke car. He was laughing so hard.
He kept trying to turn to see who was pushing him but
he couldn't make out the face. There was so much laughter. Everything was foggy behind the car. There was
someone pushing the car, but the face was obscured.
Then he heard a voice from behind the car: "Taylor, let's
get going."

He opened his eyes, dazed for a moment as the dream
faded. For a fleeting second Taylor remembered where he
knew Mike from; it was from way long ago, at Bean's, he
thought. But as his dream faded, this feeling faded.

"Time for the final climb," Mike said. "You won't
believe the view from the top of this snowfield." He was
pointing to a straight climb across this immense and open
snowfield at least a thousand feet long. It was steep, but
they'd be able to go straight up without any switchbacks.
Taylor figured it would take them at least an hour to
climb to the top, if not two. He had climbed the Muir
snowfield up at the nine thousand foot level of Mount
Rainier many times, so he knew what they were doing.

"The good news is that it will only take us ten minutes to get back down," Mike said, reading Taylor's mind
as they all stared up the snowfield in front of them.

They headed up the snowfield and climbed it, one
step at a time. Taylor was lost in thought as he climbed,
and was surprised when they were almost up to the end
of it. At the top was a view into a deep canyon, at least five
thousand feet down, and beyond into the Skychuss
Mountain peaks. Behind them Mount Baker rose out of
an endless expanse of snow-covered foothills. Taylor had
been into the mountains countless times but was still
stunned by its beauty and magnificence. The party stood
together in silence, taking in the view, everyone lost in
their own thoughts. Mark and Chris were holding hands.

Standing there, looking around in all directions at the snow-covered volcanic peak, the jagged cliffs, and the hills and valleys, Taylor had one of those perfectly peaceful, serene moments, eternally frozen in his mind. No matter where he looked, there was beauty, tranquility, and the immense power of nature. He felt so incredibly lucky to be right where he was, at that very moment. Mark and Chris were sitting atop a large boulder that had been cleared of snow. Their arms were around each other, and they stared off into the distance. Suddenly, Taylor missed Ging. He wondered what she was doing. What mundane task she was in the middle of right now? Mountain Mike was standing proudly at the edge of the cliff, staring across the giant canyon in front of him.

Then Mike turned towards the party. "It doesn't get any better than this, does it?" he said.

"Ain't that the truth," Taylor replied. He felt somewhat bonded to this new group, despite the fact that they had only met hours before. Hiking often did that.

Mark had a large smile on his face. "I want you two to be the first to know. Chris and I have just decided to get married."

"Right on, guys. I sure could see that coming," Mike said. "Actually, I thought you asked her last week when we were skiing. Congratulations."

"Congratulations," Taylor added. The thought of asking Ging to marry him suddenly seemed like the perfect thing to do. He wasn't sure if it'd still feel that way once the moment wore off and he was out of the mountains and back to Seattle. Time will tell, he told himself.

They spent about a half-hour longer at the summit they had reached. Mike had a humongous bag of trail mix that they all ate from without seeming to diminish its size. Then he began packing it up. "We'd better get going," he said.

Without anyone saying anything, they all spent several minutes in total silence, gazing all around at the wonder. Taylor was allowing every view to leave a deep imprint in his memory; he was sure the rest were doing the same.

After this, it was time to head out. Mike pulled out three squares of blue tarp material, each about four feet square. "Now for the easy part. Just put this under your butt, use your feet in front of you to keep your speed just right and you'll be down in no time. You first, Taylor."

Taylor sat on the tarp and slowly pushed himself onto the slope behind him. He slid about ten feet down, picked up a ton of speed, jammed his feet into the snow, and spun over onto his stomach, full of snow. He tried a second time and pushed his feet sooner into the snow before he picked up too much speed. This time he slid about fifty feet down the hill before he got his feet too far into the snow and ground to a sudden halt. The third time was the charm. He slid down on the tarp, yelling with glee, and kept his speed just right. Not too fast, not too slow. He made it several hundred feet down the hill before his thighs got too tired and he had to stop, simply by digging his feet in a little further. He stood up and looked up at the slope behind him. He could see Chris and Mark take off together, side by side. They obviously had done this before. They pulled up beside Taylor in no time. They watched Mike, still up at the top, pull out some kind of mini-skis from his pack, and a pair of telescoping poles, and he skied down to them.

"My newest addition," he said to them, pointing to his fat little skis. Then he took off in front of them and skied away. Mark, Chris, and Taylor followed. With more practice, Taylor was able to make it down to the bottom of the snowfield, stopping just a few times. They passed the other party Taylor had seen way behind them earlier that day. They all had a look of envy.

Mike was right. It couldn't have taken them more than fifteen minutes to get down almost a thousand feet of slope. That brought them into the valley. They hiked towards the other end of the valley. Once there, they'd just have to climb the ridge up into the parking lot. While they were going along the valley, Taylor began a conversation with Mike.

"Do you come up here a lot?" he asked him.

"Pretty often. I lead parties up here once in a while, but mostly just for fun."

Taylor realized that he hadn't paid Mike the $75 that the flyer asked for and felt a little uncomfortable raising the issue of money. "Remind me to pay you before I leave. I can be kind of a space case."

"Don't worry, guy. I love the outdoors, don't get me wrong, but I got bills; I won't forget about it. I have to admit, I can't believe this is how I make a living."

"What else do you do?"

"I teach skiing at Mt. Baker pretty often, and I work with a buddy over the summer for a whitewater rafting company. Stuff like that. Keeps me pretty busy, although I'm not sure "busy" is the right word—nor is "work" the right word."

"I see what you're saying," Taylor replied as they continued snowshoeing along the valley.

"I live in Glacier year round. It is a pretty cheap place to live so it doesn't take much to break even. And I paint. Although that I do to soothe the soul. I sell some here and there but mostly just show. Right now I have a show in Bellingham at the Galleria Expresso."

"Hey, I know that place. Right across from the hospital, right? I was just there yesterday."

"Yeah, that's the place. It's a pretty good deal. I'm friends with the owner, taught him to telemark ski. He lets me put the paintings in there and we split the money when they sell."

"Which ones are yours?" Taylor asked.

"All of them."

That surprised Taylor. The sets of paintings had looked so different he had assumed they were by several different artists. "Wow, you do all of them? They're so different...that's cool."

"Yup, I'm the 'Galleria' of the Galleria Expresso."

The conversation went into a lull and they passed into a grove of trees that signaled they were almost to the other end of the long valley. They made their way on top of the snow, through the trees, and onto a ridge that wound up at the edge of the parking lot.

They took their snowshoes off and threw them down off the bank into the snow at the edge of the parking lot. Their packs were soon to follow. Then Mark jumped down off of the bank. This was not a good idea. He sank up to his groin in the snow in the parking lot. "Better cut around," he said.

Chris, Taylor, and Mike heeded his warning and walked along the top of the bank until they found an area where they could stair step down. They all met up in the parking lot.

It had been quite a hike. Taylor was sorry it was over. He liked this bunch. Mike opened up his van and pulled out four bottles of Guinness Stout. "Tradition," he said. "Would you like one, Taylor?"

"Sure," he replied.

All four of them enjoyed a bottle of the dark Irish stout. It hit the spot. Then they began to pack up and get ready to leave. Taylor gave Mike four twenties and told him to keep the change. Mike gave him his card and said to give him a call again sometime. Taylor congratulated Chris and Mark again on their engagement and pulled his tired body into the VW. Taylor was ready to head out; Mike, Chris, and Mark were still packing up.

Taylor rolled down the window, said one last good-bye, and headed towards home, via Bellingham. He hoped to keep in touch with these guys, but he knew it'd be pretty unlikely he'd ever seen them again, especially Mark and Chris. Perhaps he could give Mountain Mike a call sometime and head up for another hike, or whitewater rafting. Ging would really enjoy it. It sounded like fun. Mike obviously knew what he was doing.

His head relaxed by the Guinness, and the sun beginning to lower in the west, Taylor headed out of the parking lot onto the winding road that dropped out of the Mount Baker Ski Resort towards Bellingham. It would be such a very long drive back home to Seattle, especially after such a long hike, that he decided to stop overnight in Bellingham.

The drive to Bellingham was so different than the reverse direction towards Mt. Baker. Where he had before been climbing along ridges and upwards into the mountains, he was now cruising downwards with a four-teen thousand-foot snow-capped peak behind him. Whereas before the snow along the roadside had steadily increased as he drove further, he now began to see increasing patches of brown until, eventually, there was no longer any snow visible. He felt the peace and serenity that he had experienced begin to wane, but he was certain that the memory of those feelings would be permanently engrained in his mind. That's how it was with enriching experiences for him. He could always retrieve them mentally and rehash them inside his head, even years later.

The sun set while he was about halfway back to Bellingham. He pulled into the parking lot of the same Best Western at about eight o'clock. It seemed like days ago since he had been there; it had just been the night before. Taylor pulled his tired and aching body out of the van, stretched for a moment, and headed into the lobby, backpack in hand, to get a room for the night. He happily remember from before that the hotel had a hot tub. He hadn't had any interest the night before in using it, but it was the first item on the agenda this day.

Taylor got a room and changed. He threw his backpack on the bed, stripped down and took a quick shower, then put on a bathing suit and headed over to the pool/hot tub room. He was relieved to see that he had the place to himself. He wasn't in much of a social mood; his body was very tired. He lowered himself into the hot tub. It was the perfect temperature. He laid his head back, closed his eyes, and enjoyed the warmth all over. Within a few minutes, he was drifting in and out of consciousness. He soaked his tired body in the hot tub for about half an hour, then got up and went back to his room. He flopped down naked on the bed and went right to sleep.

## CHAPTER NINE

# Discovery

Like the day before, no wake-up call had been needed. Taylor awoke in Bellingham, rested, around seven. The evening before, he had dozed off in the hot tub and soaked his weary body for sometime in a state of semi-consciousness, neither asleep nor awake. After that he had gone straight to his room and rolled into the bed. The clean sheets welcomed his warm body, still wet from the hot tub. He fell asleep in minutes. The night's sleep had been deep and uninterrupted. The hot tub had done the trick of rejuvenating his body. Now he hopped out of bed and quickly dressed. His mind turned to breakfast; Taylor was very hungry for a bacon and eggs breakfast. Galleria Espresso came to mind. He wanted another look at Mike's artwork, especially now that he knew that he had done all of it.

Taylor checked out and headed into town. Bellingham is one of those cities big enough to truly be called a city, yet small enough that you can park pretty much anywhere you want, anytime. He parked the van a half a block down the street from the coffee shop. As he got out of the van, he gazed across the street at the hospital. It was the last locale of his father. He thought momentarily about his father then headed into the coffee shop, his mind now switching to food.

The place was full of a mixture of people, and the mood was laid back. These were not people having morning breakfast before a day of work—this looked to be the extent of their morning plans. Or for some, a precursor to even having morning plans. Taylor liked that about Bean's: so many people just hanging out, not in a big rush to get in and out. They'd be fixtures for a time— weeks, months, sometimes even years—then suddenly vanish. He assumed their time figuring out what to do was over.

He looked around for Vicki, from the day before. It didn't appear that she was working today. Behind the counter was a Deadhead-looking girl dressed in old, tattered flannels. Working the tables was a girl that Taylor could best describe as Goth Girl: all in black, hair dyed blacker than anyone's hair could possibly be, black lipstick, dozens of hoops in one ear—quite a contrast to the upbeat hippy behind the counter. Taylor had a real problem with Goth girls. He always found their somber brooding not only annoying and disturbing, but simply bad for business. They made the worst servers and made customers feel unwanted. Being open-minded, he had hired several from this camp; all of them quit fairly quickly, saving him the uncomfortable task of firing them. Taylor had never actually had to ever fire anyone, but he always feared the situation arising.

The Grateful Dead were playing through a set of large speakers mounted on the ceiling. He assumed that the counter girl was higher on the totem pole; she got to choose the tunes. That was a privilege Taylor gave to his shift lead. It set the whole mood of the place and was quite a responsibility, not to be divvied out lightly. Taylor's head bopped along with the music and he found himself singing quietly along. "Bertha, don't you come around here anymore." Stan suddenly came to mind.

He took a table in the corner as the crowd cheered the now defunct band as they launched into "Shakedown Street." Taylor especially liked the line "Don't tell me this town ain't got no heart." The girl behind the counter began a wild, frenzied dance to the music until she knocked over a whole plate of muffins.

Goth Girl came to take his order. He assumed the upbeat music was not to her liking. She had perfected the skill of talking without any pleasantry. He ordered the bacon and eggs breakfast with the eggs scrambled, wheat toast, orange juice, and coffee. As she turned away, he heard her humming along with the music ever so quietly to herself.

Taylor looked around at the artwork covering the back walls. There was much more of it than he had noticed the night before. He scanned the wall as the Dead launched into a long, driving jam. His eyes kept coming back to the set showing what looked to be a family of three, with one parent in black and white and the other parent and the child in color. He got up to get a closer look. There was little detail to the faces but he could see that the child was a young boy and the parent in black and white silhouette was a woman, the other parent, in color, was a man. The father and the son appeared happily playing away in the paintings, the mother, off in the distance, glaring unhappily. He felt that perhaps he was looking at his own family, so many years ago. The prices were on a small card underneath each painting. Most were $50. Taylor decided to buy one and approached the girl at the counter who was once again dancing. The muffins were back on the plate. He had sworn that they had landed on the ground. He was glad he didn't order any muffins.

She stopped dancing as he approached.

"Hi, I'd like to buy one of those paintings on the wall," he said

"Right on," she said matter-of-factly. "Just go grab the one you want and bring it up here. I'll ring it up."

Taylor went over and chose one that had really caught his eye. In it, the dad was pushing the boy in a tricycle with the mom glaring at them off in the distance. He brought it up to the counter, pulled out his credit card, and paid for it. As he was paying, he noticed Goth Girl placing his order on his table. Taylor paid for the painting and, with it in hand, returned to his table for breakfast.

The food hit the spot. He ate his breakfast quietly while the Dead transitioned into a lively version of "Truckin.'" With his plate clean, Taylor slapped a ten-dollar bill on the table and got up to leave. It would be a tip larger than the unfriendly waitress deserved, but it would be worth it to him not to have to deal with her again for change. He picked up his painting and headed out the door to drive home to Seattle.

It would be an easy drive. Interstate 5, or I-5 as it is known, runs straight from Bellingham to Seattle. Actually it runs all the way from the Canadian to the Mexican Border. The speed limit on the stretch he would be traveling was 70 mph most of the way, thanks to the Republican revolution of the '90s. Once on the freeway and at cruising speed, Taylor opened his glove compartment where he had some more CD's than the few he brought. He got out a Neil Young CD, Live Rust, and put it on. With music playing, he drove the hundred miles south in no time.

The only stop he made was at one of the rest areas, for the "free" coffee. Even though the coffee was watered down, it hit the spot. He put a few quarters in the donation jar for whatever charity was running it. He grabbed a few cookies and a cup of coffee and drank it at a picnic table off to the side. The charity running the rest stop was

a little league baseball team; the parents were very friendly.


Before he knew it, Taylor passed the northern city limits
of Seattle. The Friday mid-day traffic was light. He got
off the freeway at the University of Washington exit, 45th
Street—The Ave. The parking angel was smiling on him
as he saw a car leaving right in front of Bean's as he pulled
up. He parked and went in.

Roger was behind the counter. Things seemed in
control. Taylor trusted Roger and hadn't worried whatso-
ever about things back home while he was gone.

"Hey Tay, how's it goin', guy?" Roger said. He always
called Taylor "Tay."

"All right. How'd things go?"

"No problems. People come in. We take their money
and give them coffee, food, and a place to hang. They pay,
leave, and come back. You know the routine."

"Roger, I really appreciate your looking after the place
while I was gone. Ironically, I wound up being in charge
because I was looking after the place when Stan was
gone." It was a legendary story that everyone had heard.

"Thanks for not doing that to me. You settle things up
there?" Roger asked with a hint of curiosity.

"I think so. It was some old left-over stuff about my
dad." Taylor and Roger had talked about the whole thing
occasionally, so he didn't think he had to fill him in any
further. "I did buy a cool painting for my apartment. I
snowshoed with the artist and bought a painting by him
in Bellingham afterwards."

"Cool," Roger said.

"Yeah, it really connected with me for some reason,"
Taylor said. "Can you cover the rest of the day? I'll cover
your weekend shifts."

"No prob. Sounds like a good trade to me," Roger replied. He usually worked Saturday and Sunday and had Tuesday and Wednesday off. While he never complained about it, he was hoping soon to pass that responsibility on to someone else and get off the weekends. This would be a good start. Taylor called Ging from the office to tell her he was back. She sounded real happy to hear from him. He responded to her "How did it all go?" inquiry with a "Fine, babe. I can fill you in when I get there." He told her he had missed her and was really looking forward to seeing her. Taylor got off the phone and got ready to leave.

"All right, Rog, see you next week. Have a good weekend off. Let's talk next week about you getting a few weekends a month off." Taylor was good at reading his employees and dealing with issues before they really became issues.

"Sure thing, Tay. I'd like that. I'm sure that someone new would jump at the chance of being in charge of a weekend. I know I sure went for it big time."

"Yup, I remember that. How about you split it with someone else; you do every other weekend for a start. Then, if it works out, you can turn it over."

"That'd be good."

"See you next week," Taylor said as he headed out the door. "And put on some tunes. This place is dead."


Taylor left his car where it was—good spots are hard to come by—and started walking to his apartment. It was a short walk. About halfway there, he remembered the painting. He really wanted to show up with it to surprise Ging. He stopped for a moment, like a squirrel in the middle of the road, trying to decide whether to head on without the painting or go back and get it. He turned around and headed back to his van, got the painting, and walked down The Ave towards his apartment, painting in hand. He liked how everyone he passed would take a look at the painting. A few people made comments, all positive. It wasn't until he was heading up the stairs to his place that it occurred to him that some of the passersby may have mistaken him for the artist, not the owner.

"Honey, I'm home," he said as he came through the door.

Ging came running at him, arms open, ready to throw him a big hug. She had a big, warm smile for him. He put the painting down and they embraced and kissed.

"Man, it is great to see you," she said. "Can I get you a beer? How did it go?"

"Sure, I'd love a beer."

Ging went to the fridge and came back with a Heineken. "Here, you can have my Heiney, honey," she said playfully. It was an overused joke borrowed from a recently popular movie. It made Taylor laugh anyway. They took a seat together on the couch. Taylor filled her in on everything since he had left on Sunday: the partied-out kids at the rest stop on the way up, the Galleria Expresso, the girl, Vicki, who used to work for him, the hospital, snowshoeing, and the painting.

"Let me check it out," Ging said about the painting. It was leaning against the wall with its back showing. She was curious about it and was waiting for him to get to it. She caught just a glimpse of it as he came in the door; it gave her an odd feeling.

Taylor picked up the painting and flipped it around. Ging got a sudden, surprised look on her face and she immediately said, without thinking, "Your dad painted this."

Taylor was puzzled. "No way. I know the guy who painted this and trust me, he's not my dad."

"Taylor, your dad painted this."

"What are you talking about? What makes you say that?" He got a sudden tightening feeling in his stomach. Deep down, he got what she was telling him, but on the surface, it seemed absurd.

"Look, Taylor, I don't want to make a big deal out of this. Remember the first time we met. I told you I was for real. It doesn't happen too often but when it does, it is for real."

Taylor didn't say anything. She had told Stan that Jerry Garcia was going to die and that turned out to be true—easily explainable as a lucky guess. He did remember the first time they met, how she told him his father wasn't dead. That turned out to be true. That was freaky and by no means a lucky guess. There were other times too. She'd seem like she had something but wouldn't tell him. Once she told him she'd discovered that it was easier to keep it to herself and he didn't press her. Now this—what to make of this?

"Let me get this straight. Are you saying that my dad painted this instead of the guy I went snowshoeing with, or that the guy I went snowshoeing with is my dad?"

"All's I know is that your dad painted this," she replied. "I say we head straight back up there and find this guy. This time, please, can I go with you?" She emphasized the word please.

"Damn," Taylor said, thinking of the deal he made with Roger. "I can't go until Monday. I gotta work this weekend."

"Then let's go Monday," she said. "It'll wait."

"No, it can't," he said. "I can get someone else to watch the store for the weekend. Perks of being a good boss. Roger is my first choice but I can have Emily keep an eye on things. She's working today and all weekend. I can swing by, spend a few hours taking care of some things, then take off. She'll be fine. But I have to get going. I'll be back in a few hours and we can take off tonight."

"All right, I'll have dinner waiting for you," she said.

"Deal," Taylor replied and headed out the door. He stopped momentarily and looked at the painting. He knew she was right. Now he understood that unexplainable feeling he had when he looked at the painting: the son and dad in color; the woman a shadow in the background. The feeling he knew Mike from along time ago and the strange looks Mike had given him both came back to Taylor.

He took off running towards Bean's. With luck, he could be in and out of there in not much more than an hour. A sudden idea came to mind; Emily would be a perfect choice to split running the weekends with Roger. She had been working for him for over a year, never missed a day, and everyone loved her. She was some kind of an aspiring writer, always talking about a book she was working on. He talked briefly with her about it and she was ecstatic. It'd mean more money and more importantly, she said, she really felt like she was ready for more responsibility. It seemed like a win-win-win situation for him, Emily, and Roger. Taylor could get the weekend off, Emily could start on her every-other-weekend shift, and Roger could get some weekends off. He loved when things worked out like this. They often did for him.

In the office, he looked over the inventory, receipts, and orders. Roger had done a perfect job. He had put all the bills in the "to be paid" file, logged all the baked goods and coffee beans that came in on the appropriate place, and all the completed timecards were in the right spot, none missing. He knew that Roger must have had to bug several people to fill out their timecards; Taylor always had to do that each week without fail. He was real impressed at the job Roger had done and made a mental note to both mention this and line up Roger to show the ropes to Emily. It would give Roger a good sense of recognition. Taylor went into the "to be paid" folder and wrote checks for all the bills nearing due, stamped the envelopes, and went outside and dropped them into the mailbox. He hated the feeling of mail ready to go out, sitting around. He went back to the office and signed and processed everyone's time cards and filled out the payroll sheet for the bank. This too he put in an envelope, addressed, stamped, and dropped in the mailbox outside. Everyone would be getting their paychecks on time. He left the office and made himself a double macchiato and sat down for a moment. He looked at his watch. It'd been only forty minutes since he'd come in and he'd lined up Emily for the weekend and taken care of all the details.

"Damn, I'm good," he said to himself, enjoying his coffee drink. He'd come a long way since his first days there. He looked around with a sense of pride. Bean's was quite full and had a real relaxing energy about it. He felt that this was his signature on the place. When he first started working there, it was kind of chaotic inside. Not a place to come in and relax. It felt like all the tensions from the outside were brought in with the customers. Now, it was a place to chill and leave the baggage outside.

He finished his coffee and got up to leave. "Good luck, Emily, you'll do great," he said to her on his way out.

"Thanks a bunch, see you Monday," she replied. "The place is in good hands."

Taylor left Bean's and headed home. There'd be plenty of time to load up and get to Bellingham before it got too late. They could get a room for the night and be up bright and early Saturday morning to look for Mike. It seemed surreal, the whole thing. He didn't really have an idea of what to do except to head up to Bellingham and find Mike. It would be easy. He'd called several times from Bean's and got a recording each time. He didn't leave a message the first few times then finally left his name and number and said he'd like to hook up again and asked Mike to call him.

On the way home he remembered Ging saying she'd make them dinner, but he felt too impatient to sit down and eat a meal. Ging was a great cook and he didn't want to be rude. When she cooked, she let out all the stops and made a great meal and mood. He'd just bite the bullet on this one.

He walked in the door and was confused: no candles lit on the table, no romantic music playing on the stereo, the table wasn't set, no delicious aroma filling the apartment. Ging came out of the bedroom with a backpack.

"Everything is ready to go. I made us some rice and bean wraps to eat on the way up. I packed your stuff for you; let's get going."

Taylor felt how happy he was that she was joining him on what he figured was the last part of this long journey. She had been so patient and understanding that he was doing much of this alone, even though she was the one who got the whole ball rolling.

"Man, you are the coolest," he said, giving her a big hug. "I don't think I could do this without you." He meant it but he didn't really know what "this" meant. "I'm going to need some help figuring out what do to up there. We can talk about it on the way up."

He called Mike's number before leaving but, once again, there was no answer.

"Let's get a room in Bellingham for the night, then head up to Glacier tomorrow first thing. Mike said he lives there, and it's a real tiny town just before Mt. Baker. We can ask around. I'm sure the locals will know him.

There is a sport shop, general store, and a couple of restaurants there."

"Sounds like a plan to me," Ging said. She gave him a kiss and said, "Thanks for having me along."

"You're most welcome. What do you think I should say to him?" he asked.

"Good question. There's the direct approach and the indirect approach. Should we flip a coin?"

"I'm figuring we can play it by ear. Ask him a few questions. See if he starts acting weird and suspicious. Maybe just blurt it out. Who knows? Maybe he doesn't even know who he is."

"Good point."

They grabbed the bag Ging had packed and the paper bag with the dinner for the road, and headed out. In the hallway they passed a set of fire department aid guys. They looked familiar as they passed them on their way to the apartment at the end of the hallway. Ging and Taylor gave each other a look and chucked as they headed out. Hand in hand, they walked up The Ave towards Bean's, where the van was parked. Taylor did a U-turn and headed north towards I-5 and Bellingham.

Ging popped in a CD she had brought for the road, Sarah McLaughlin. The first song was melodic and the opening line was "Hold on, hold on to yourself, cause this is going to hurt like hell."

## CHAPTER TEN

# A Close Encounter

The Friday night traffic north out of Seattle was light. On the other side of I-5 they could see a massive parking lot of a backup heading the other direction into the city. Traffic northward was cruising out of the city unimpeded. A light mist began falling as they passed the northern limits of Seattle. Beyond Seattle to the north, the freeway is lined with expanses of evergreen trees. They passed through Everett, the last city north of Seattle for some time.

As always, Taylor stopped at rest stops for the coffee and cookies. This was a tradition for him. He put a handful of quarters into the collection container, an empty can of Maxwell House coffee with a slit cut in the plastic top. The coins jingled as they hit the bottom. A 4-H group was manning the rest stop, a collection of older women and young teenage girls. The girls had that wide-hipped look of horse riders, and were all giggling together at something. One of the old ladies thanked Taylor and asked him if he wanted anything in his coffee.

"No thanks," he replied. Ging had headed into the bathroom, and Taylor was left holding two cups of coffee waiting for her. "How you guys doing tonight, busy?" he asked.

"Sure thing," the three older ladies all answered in unison.

Taylor continued the polite small talk with them until Ging came out. "Well, I gotta get going. Thanks a lot, see you, good luck the rest of the day," he said as he walked to join Ging, two coffees in one hand and a couple of cookies palmed into the other. He had an uplifting, warm feeling from patronizing the fundraiser.

They got back in the van and drove, without stopping, the remaining ninety minutes to Bellingham. They talked while he drove. The general plan they arrived at was to get a room for the night in Bellingham, call Mountain Mike as soon as they got there, and again in the morning if they didn't get a hold of him. Taylor would tell him he had a great time snowshoeing, was back north, and needed to come by and talk with him about something. Mike seemed like an all right guy, and there shouldn't be any need for any big story. If all else failed, he'd talk with him over the phone, but he really wanted to see him in person. In the event that they couldn't get a hold of him, they'd drive towards Mount Baker, stop off in Glacier, and ask around at the snow sports shop, the convenience store, or the restaurant until they found someone who could help them. Taylor assumed that since it was such a tiny town and Mike was a local, they wouldn't have to go any further than asking at the first place. They agreed that the snow sports shop made the most sense to start with.

Before they knew it, they passed a sign that said five miles until Bellingham. The mist had turned into a steady rain. The wipers streaked across the windshield. Taylor got off the freeway at the exit for the same Best Western he had stayed at just the night before—it didn't seem possible…it seemed like weeks ago. The girl at the desk gave him an inquisitive look when he asked for a room for the night. She was the same girl that had checked him in Thursday night, and probably imagined all sorts of possibilities as to why he was checking in again, this time with a girl, a gorgeous, sexy one nonetheless. Taylor gave Ging a wink and said, "Lookie what I found." The girl behind the counter did not looked amused.

"For the record, I found him," Ging said, directed at no one in particular.

The first thing Taylor did when he got to the room was to flop down on the bed.

"Man, I'm beat," he said. "They have a hot tub...how does that sound?"

"You read my mind," Ging replied. She peeled off her clothes and changed into her bathing suit. She could see Taylor checking her out as she undressed with her back turned to him. She paused, wearing nothing but her thong. He didn't realize that she could see him though the mirror, staring at her. She felt good, due both to his attention and her teasing him a little. He went into the bathroom and changed into his bathing suit. For some reason, he was embarrassed to change in front of her and have her see his huge erection. He thought he had just had a secret voyeur moment. It didn't occur to him that she was giving him a show.

Bathing suits on, they walked hand in hand down the hall to the pool room and slid into the hot tub together. Taylor sat in the hot tub and Ging leaned back into his lap, her head laying on his shoulder, his arms wrapped around her. Taylor leaned forward, kissed Ging on the ear, and whispered "I love you" sweetly to her.

"Love you too," she replied.

They relaxed in the hot tub for almost an hour, occasionally getting out to cool off, then toweled dry and went back up to the room. As soon as the door closed behind them Taylor pushed Ging up against it and pulled her suit off. "Ohhhh, yeah," Ging moaned. She reached out and pulled his trunks off. They made love, first with her up against the door, and then walked hand in hand to the bed, where they continued. All the stress of the past twenty-four hours evaporated away and, around midnight, they were fast asleep in each other's arms.

Morning came fast. Taylor awoke from a strange dream—a man and a woman fighting while a little boy looked on from behind a partially opened door. Fog obscured all the details. The dream seemed crystal clear and vivid upon the moment of awakening, but quickly faded.

He got up and looked out the hotel window. The sun was rising and a beautiful sunrise was painted across the sky. Violent reds and oranges streaked over the horizon.

"Morning honey," Ging said from the bed. She was naked, propped upright supported by her elbows.

"I just had the weirdest dream," Taylor said.

"Oh yeah, what was so weird about it?"

Taylor paused. "That's strange. I feel like I remembered it just then, but now it's gone. Oh, well."

He picked up the phone and dialed the number for Mountain Mike. No answer, just an answering machine. He didn't leave a message.

"Come on. Let's just head up there," he said to Ging.

They checked out and got on highway twenty towards Glacier and Mount Baker. They didn't talk much on the way there. At some point Ging fell asleep. Within an hour they were pulling into the town of Glacier. Glacier barely constitutes a town, more like a cluster of cabins nestled in the woods on either side of the North Cascades Highway, less than an hour from the Mount Baker ski area. The actual center of the town is a group of four buildings, two on either side of the road. On one side was an Italian restaurant and a gas station with an attached convenience store. On the other was a mountain sports shop and a tavern. There wasn't even a traffic light.

Taylor pulled into the parking lot of the sports shop. Outside was a payphone. He dropped in a quarter and dialed the number for Mountain Mike. A voice on the phone instructed him to drop in a quarter. He noticed the sticker on the phone, fifty cents per call.

"When did a phone call become fifty cents?" he muttered to himself, sounding like a grouchy old man.

The phone rang, but again there was no answer, just an answering machine. Again, he didn't leave a message. He put in another fifty cents and dialed again, this time intending to leave a message. At the beep, he hung up. He became lost in thought for several moments. The dream from the night before seemed to be creeping back into his mind—sort of a déjà vu feeling. He was on the verge of remembering it.

"No answer?" Ging said, breaking his train of thought, bringing him back.

"No. Let's go inside and ask."

They went inside the sports shop. It was a rustic old place, constructed long ago from massive wooden beams. The store was jammed with all sorts of mountain sports gear: skis, snowboards, mountain-climbing gear, and clothes. Up front, one of those old-fashioned counters made from glass was manned by an outdoorsy kind of guy wearing a flannel shirt. He looked like one of those people who spend their whole life enjoying recreation and funding it with some kind of day job centered on their hobbies.

Taylor approached him and asked politely, "Excuse me, can you tell me how to get a hold of Mike?"

The expression of the guy behind the counter changed slightly to a mildly threatening look. He gave Taylor a hard glare. "You a friend of his?"

"Not really, I just need to talk to him about something."

The man replied, "Well, he ain't here."

"Do you know how I can get hold of him?"

"I said he ain't here. I already said that," he said somewhat impatiently. Taylor didn't understand all the sudden hostility.

"What's the deal? I just want to talk to him," Taylor said mildly.

"Sorry, I can't help you," was the response, sounding a little calmer.

Taylor left his number with the guy and asked him to give it to Mike if he saw him. On the way back to the van he remembered that Mike had mentioned that he lived in a cabin behind the shop. Taylor told Ging to wait in the van for a minute and he walked around back. He told her he needed to go to the bathroom. There was a single cabin in the woods, a hundred feet back. It was the only one anywhere around there. It had to be the cabin Mike was referring to. He walked back into the woods towards the cabin.

It was a small, single-level cabin. Taylor peered in through one of the windows. The inside was well kept, obviously lived-in. He went around and knocked on the door: no answer. He tried the doorknob out of sheer chance, but it was locked. Intent on getting inside to look around, Taylor went around to the back. After trying a few windows, he found one that he could pry open. He climbed up and slipped inside.

"Hello, anyone here?" he said a few times. No one answered.

Taylor looked around the abandoned cabin. He found a few outdoor magazines addressed to Mike. He was in the right place. He began looking feverishly through drawers, in cabinets, not sure what he was searching for. He didn't find much.

Suddenly the front door burst open and in came the flannel guy from the sports shop, accompanied by a much larger man with a gun in his hands. They looked quite threatening.

"OK, pal, just what do you think you're doing?" the flannel guy asked threateningly.

Normally a quick thinker, Taylor stared back silently. Finally, after a few moments of the stand-off, he began to try talking his way out of this.

"Look, you're probably not going to believe this, but I'll be straight with you anyway: Mike's my dad and—"

"Bullshit. I'm calling the cops," interrupted the larger man with the gun. He picked up the phone and dialed. "Todd, we need you over at Mike's cabin right away, behind the store. We just caught some guy breaking in. I think he'll be able to fill us in on Mike. Get over here right away," he said into the phone.

In a micro-town like Glacier, "right away" really must mean right away because Todd showed up in about sixty seconds. He was a county cop.

The cop instantly took charge. "I'm officer Justice," he said to Taylor. "Now, do you want to tell me what you're doing in someone else's cabin?"

"Officer Justice. You got to be kidding me," Taylor said. It seemed to lighten up the mood.

"Look, you're in a lot of trouble, sir," The officer responded.

Just then, Ging peered in the open front door. "Everything OK in here?" she asked meekly.

"Come on in, babe," Taylor said to her.

She came in and stood by Taylor.

"What's going on?" she asked.

"This is Mike's cabin. I came in to have a look around," Taylor replied.

Officer Justice stepped forward. "OK, now just tell us what you're doing breaking and entering into someone else's cabin?"

Taylor told them how his dad had vanished years ago and he just recently found out Mike was his dad. He was somewhat vague about how this discovery came about. He gave only as much detail as was needed. They did seem to give him a chance and began buying his story. The tension seemed to slowly dissolve away.

"I'm sorry to have broken into his cabin. I guess I should have just waited for him to return my call," Taylor said. "Am I under arrest?"

Officer Justice gave Taylor a hard look. "Not at this point," he said.

"Can you explain things to Mike when you see him and have him give me a call?" Taylor asked. "I'll give you my number."

All three men seemed like they were waiting for one of them to say something. Finally, the guy from the shop spoke up.

"Well, that's just it. It seems that Mike bugged-out and just up and took off yesterday. A friend of ours ran into him and said Mike was all in a panic, said someone was coming after him. Didn't make a lot of sense. Just said he had to be going and told him to tell everyone goodbye. Said he'd be back when things blew over. We have no idea what it was about. Are you sure you can't shed some light on it?"

"Sorry, but I can't," Taylor replied, relieved that he seemed to be clear of being in trouble.

The officer asked for Taylor's ID and left for a few moments to go to his cruiser to check him out.

"I'll be right back," he said. "You'd better hope you come up clean."

While he was gone Taylor talked with the flannel guy, whose name turned out to be Rob; his larger partner's name was Andy. Rob told Taylor he had been a good friend of Mike's for a long time and was very worried about him.

Rob told him how he had come to know Mike. It all seemed to fit into the picture that was evolving, coming clearer. Mike had come into town one summer years ago, and the talk was that he'd been living in a tent up in the woods for a few weeks. Everyone figured he was some kind of a fugitive, and they were relieved when he turned out to be harmless—actually, quite nice. Mike had told them he was on his way to Canada to live with his brother, but no one had really believed him. It didn't matter. Up in Glacier, no one asked too many questions. Rob, who owned the sport shop, befriended Mike pretty quickly. Mike began working there in exchange for staying in the cabin in back and a small cash salary. Rob had bought the cabin along with the store but already had a place to live. He rented it out occasionally, but that was always kind of more work than it was worth. It was usually empty.

After Rob got to know him, Mike told him that he'd been in some kind of an accident and had lost most his memory; he'd come up to Glacier to try to sort it out and start over. He didn't think that Mike ever sorted it out, but he sure started over. Rob thought it didn't seem to serve any purpose to ask too many questions. Rob helped him get a fake social security number and ID so that he could legitimately have Mike work for him. Rob wasn't even sure what his real name was. Mike seemed to have no interest in looking into his past. Whenever his past got brought up, he seemed very uncomfortable.

Mike was quite an outdoorsman. He worked at the shop and began a side business guiding rafting trips, hikes, and summit climbs to Mount Baker. Eventually that became enough of a business that he worked less and less in the store. He bought the cabin from Rob and had lived in it since. Rob sold it to him for half of what it was worth. In return, Mike sent all sorts of business to the sport shop. It was a good deal for both. Mike had become a fixture in Glacier and joined the small group of year-round inhabitants of the town. They didn't talk about the past with him much, after the first few years.

The cop came back in and said Taylor and Ging could leave. Taylor left his business card from Bean's and asked them to give it to Mike if they saw him and to explain the whole thing. They agreed they'd do that.

"Hopefully, he'll come back," Rob said. "We'll hook you guys up. Give it some time."


Taylor and Ging drove out of Glacier towards Bellingham. They contemplated staying in Glacier for a few days, but it seemed doubtful that Mike would be returning anytime soon. The drive back to Bellingham was beautiful. Mountains lined both sides of the North Cascades Highway. Once at Bellingham they got onto I-5 and cruised southward to Seattle, making the required stops for the free watered-down coffee. Ging rolled her eyes every time he pulled over. She humored him by drinking the watered-down coffee.

"Taylor, how can someone who makes a living selling espresso enjoy this stuff?"

"I just love helping out," he replied. "I just made those kids' baseball team fifty cents richer."

Ging smiled. Taylor was so generous and giving. It was a nice quality.

The next day, in the late afternoon, Taylor went out to Bean's to check in. He wanted to make sure everything had gone well in his absence. It always did. He walked into the café—all looked well. There were two kids in the corner playing chess. A group of girls at another table appeared to be studying together. Taylor's old German Literature professor, Dr. Heintz, was sitting quietly with his wife at another table, towards the door. His was the last class he had taken. It'd been several years ago. Taylor had made a strong and lasting impression on the professor, always asking excellent questions and contributing to any discussions they were having in class.

He looked up as Taylor walked by.

"Hello, Taylor. How's it going? Long time, no see," Dr. Heintz said with a heavy German accent. Taylor was surprised to be remembered.

"Guten Tag, Doctor Heintz. Wie geitz?" he replied respectfully. "How go your German studies?"

"Pretty good, Taylor. How have you been doing? I don't see you anymore on campus. I was hoping to see you in my Germen Lit Two class."

"I'm taking a hiatus. I've been running the café full time."

"Hmmm, that's too bad. Well, you're quite talented. I'm sure you'll do well with whatever you do. I hope you consider coming back someday. You're such a gifted student—so much more perceptive than most. I can remember how excited you'd get in class. I wish I had more students like you. Your absence is the University's loss."

"Thanks, that is very kind of you," Taylor responded. Just then, he noticed someone talking to Charlotte, the barista who was also running the counter. He looked oddly familiar from behind. Charlotte looked a little uneasy, like the man might be bothering her.

"Nice talking with you, Doctor Heintz. Sorry, but I have to go," Taylor said, his attention focused on the espresso counter. Charlotte was looking Taylor's way with a pleading look in her eyes, motioning him over. Taylor approached to help out. It was pretty rare— beyond rare—for someone to hassle a barista. There was a first for everything.

"Is there a problem?" Taylor said, with as much authority in his voice as he could muster. He tensed up, preparing for trouble.

The man who had been talking to Charlotte had Taylor's business card in his hand. He turned around and faced Taylor. It was Mountain Mike. It was his father.

## CHAPTER ELEVEN

# Reunions

Time froze. Freeze frame. Taylor and Mountain Mike stood, staring at each other, two feet apart, face to face. Father and son. Mike dropped Taylor's business card to the floor, staring at his son. He was the first to break the silence.

"I don't remember you. You need to understand that," he said slowly. "I might be your father, but if I can't remember it, what would that even mean?"

Taylor didn't know what to say. "I'd like to get to know you," was all he could come up with.

"Me, too," Mike replied—a double meaning, as he didn't really know himself or Taylor. "I can't really remember anything from before coming to Glacier."

Then, all of a sudden, an isolated memory tried to drift back to the father: a fleeting memory of him, Taylor, and Taylor's mother. It floated in like a breeze in the night and was gone as quickly as it came.

"Maybe it'll come back. Will you please help me remember it?" Taylor's dad asked him.

He reached out and embraced his son. Taylor held him tight.

"Mom told me you were dead. I grew up thinking you had died."

"No, I didn't die. Not really."

Mike went on to tell Taylor how he had come back to his cabin the previous night to grab some of his things. He was on the run. From what, he didn't know. Coming face to face with Taylor must have awoken some long-lost panic inside him. He actually thought he was going crazy. His friend, Rob, was waiting for him in his cabin. Rob explained the whole thing to him. It took him awhile to calm Mike down and convince him to not flee. He convinced him to come down to Seattle to meet Taylor. Mike couldn't remember any of his past before Glacier. Now, after meeting his son, it seemed for the first time that he could unlock the mystery of the missing first half of his life.

"How is your mother?" he asked Taylor. "She must have wondered all these years what became of me. Did she think I left her? Were we happy together?"

Taylor thought for a moment. "Mom died of cancer last year. She had told me you died in a car crash. I'll never know what she really thought." He didn't want to go into any of the details now, or ever, for that matter.

"It must have been hard for you," Mike said to his son. "Man, I don't have any memories of her."

"Yeah, it was hard, but we got by all right. You had life insurance. She learned to take care of me alone. I always felt she missed you. Can I get you something?" he asked his father.

Taylor's dad replied, "How about a coffee?"

He got his dad a coffee and they sat at a table in the corner. Taylor told his dad about his childhood, his adolescence, going off to college, taking over Bean's. His dad listened intently, pride developing over the son he never knew. His father filled him in on his life in Glacier. Some of it Rob had already told to Taylor, but he enjoyed hearing it first hand. Mike had married again, after settling in

Glacier, but his wife died years ago in a climbing accident on Mount McKinley in Alaska. He'd been alone since then.

Finally, Taylor's dad asked, "Taylor, do you know what happened to me? I did some hypnosis years ago. They told me that I had been kidnapped, put in a trunk, and injured by jumping out of the moving car. I didn't really buy it. Sounded too much like a movie I might have seen."

"That's more than I know, Dad," Taylor said.

"Who the heck would have kidnapped me?" he said rhetorically.

How does one recapture a life of lost time? Taylor and his father talked into the evening, up until closing time. After he closed up Bean's, Taylor walked with his dad to his apartment. Ging was waiting there with a late spaghetti dinner for them. Taylor had called her from Bean's, explained the whole thing, and asked her to be there. He'd told his dad all about Ging.

Ging gave Taylor's dad a warm hug when he came in.

"Nice to meet you," she said politely.

"Likewise," Mike replied. "I understand we have you to thank for bringing us together."

"Well, me and many others," she said. "Really, most the credit goes to Taylor."

Mike looked up at his painting hanging on the wall. He seemed somewhat puzzled.

Taylor saw his dad looking at the painting.

"I bought that up in Bellingham last week after we snowshoed. Look familiar?"


Taylor's dad stayed with them for a week. How quickly the years came back. They felt comfortable together, father and son. The huge gap of missing years dissolved away as they spent time together, even though none of his father's lost memories returned.

At the end of the week, Taylor's dad told him he was going to return to Glacier. That was where his life was. They made tentative plans to climb Mount Baker the following summer.

Taylor said goodbye, but promised to get up to Glacier regularly; His dad promised to get down to Seattle. It all seemed pretty genuine. On the day his father left, Taylor felt both sad and happy.

A few weeks went by. Taylor's life went back to normal. He spoke with his father by phone once a week or so and was making plans to go up and see him soon. Life at Bean's was going smoothly.

Late one Sunday evening, when Taylor was putting together the next month's schedule and doing some of the bookkeeping, a tall, skinny, bald middle-aged man came into the café. He walked right up to Taylor and said, "A blast from the past."

Taylor looked up, at first in puzzlement without an ounce of recognition, then a huge smile exploded over his face.

"Stan! Stan, how the HELL are you!" He jumped out and threw his arms around his former big brother.

The road had been hard on Stan. He looked like he had lost quite a lot of weight. His shaved head made him almost unrecognizable to his old friend.

"I'm back," Stan said. "Looks like the place is still standing."

"It's still standing all right. What the hell have you been up to?" Taylor said. "I thought I'd never see you again."

"Well. I was on the road following the Dead. You got my postcards, didn't you?"

"Yeah, we got them."

"Things were getting kind of rowdy at the concerts. A mixture of the loyal and all these younger kids, they were kind of out of hand. Can you imagine that, rowdy Grateful Dead concerts? There were too many people who didn't belong there. The shows got kind of spotty."

"I heard about that."

"I hung out in Chicago with some old friends after the last shows. We were hoping things would be better when the tour started up again. But then Jerry died. We all went to the memorial in Golden Gate Park."

"How was that?"

"It was quite a scene. After that, I moved to Phoenix and worked for a friend of mine remodeling houses. Things just weren't the same. I started getting insomnia and I went a long time without sleep. I think I had a nervous breakdown. My friends convinced me to go into the hospital for a while. I was in the psych ward for sometime."

"Really?"

"Yeah. Then I left Phoenix with some guys I worked with and we followed Phish around for a while, but it wasn't the same. I went back to San Francisco and spent some time there. Then, for some reason I'll never understand until the end of time, I joined up with the Hare Krishnas. It seemed to make perfect sense at the time. I did that for over a year. It was actually good for me. When the time came where I was ready to leave, they all supported me. I've been down in Portland for a while, regrouping. Now I'm back here. My hair should grow back within a few months. I've still been shaving it. Don't say it. I know I look like crap."

"No denying that," Taylor replied. "Dude, the Hare Krishnas?"

"Yeah, I know. Who'd of thunk it? I don't know what the heck I was doing. I guess I was just looking for answers," Stan said.

"Did you hang out at the airport and give out flowers?"

"Yup, many times."

"What are your plans now?" Taylor asked.

"Well, I was hoping to come back to Bean's to start?"

"Ray was kind of pissed at you. But he doesn't come around at all. I don't know if you know this, but I took over your job. I'm the top honcho now. Stan, I believe you were fired."

"So, you do the hiring, right?" Stan said with a smile.

"Yup, and I have a good feeling about you, young man." Taylor said.